She felt it now—the same mindless attraction

Laurel's soft mouth tightened as she recalled the pain and humiliation that had followed that initial stupidity.

Never again. The year she had spent in hell had made her so deeply suspicious of desire that she had vowed never to fall beneath its spell again. She thought she had managed to repress all feeling, until, through an open doorway, she had seen a man who bore a strong resemblance to the husband who had stripped her confidence from her with petulant cruelty.

But then, how good a judge of personality was she? She had thought Martin had loved her, that he had had it in him to be a tender man, a good husband and father. And she'd been so wrong.

Could she be wrong about Alick, too?

ROBYN DONALD lives in northern New Zealand with her husband and children. They love the outdoors and particularly enjoy sailing and stargazing on warm nights. Robyn doesn't remember being taught to read, but rates reading as one of her greatest pleasures, if not a vice. She finds writing intensely rewarding and is continually surprised by the way her characters develop independent lives of their own.

Books by Robyn Donald

HARLEQUIN PRESENTS
1263—A BITTER HOMECOMING
1303—NO GUARANTEES
1343—A MATTER OF WILL
1376—THE DARKER SIDE OF PARADISE
1408—A SUMMER STORM
1434—NO PLACE TOO FAR

HARLEQUIN ROMANCE
2391—BAY OF STARS
2437—ICEBERG

Don't miss any of our special offers. Write to us at the following address for information on our newest releases.

Harlequin Reader Service
P.O. Box 1397, Buffalo, NY 14240
Canadian address: P.O. Box 603,
Fort Erie, Ont. L2A 5X3

ROBYN DONALD

some kind of madness

Harlequin Books

TORONTO • NEW YORK • LONDON
AMSTERDAM • PARIS • SYDNEY • HAMBURG
STOCKHOLM • ATHENS • TOKYO • MILAN
MADRID • WARSAW • BUDAPEST • AUCKLAND

Dedicated with love to
Molly and Douglas Kingston,
my parents-in-law, whose wonderful
diamond wedding celebrations
gave me the idea for this book.

And in loving memory of my father,
Ian Hutching,
who enjoyed their party so much, and
who died before I finished the manuscript.

Harlequin Presents first edition June 1992
ISBN 0-373-11464-8

Original hardcover edition published in 1991
by Mills & Boon Limited

SOME KIND OF MADNESS

CHAPTER ONE

'OF COURSE you'll have to go.'

When Mrs Webster spoke in that plaintive tone her daughter, who was gazing at her with something like horror, felt a spasm of pain and sympathy lance through her. Her objections died on her lips.

However, it was not in Laurel's character to give up easily. 'But I'm not going to know a soul there. I've never been further north of Auckland than Whangarei, certainly not up as far as Kerikeri. Until five minutes ago, I didn't even know we had relatives there! I'll be totally out of place at a diamond wedding anniversary, even if it is being celebrated by my great-aunt and her husband.'

But her mother had clearly prepared herself for protests. 'Kerikeri is a pretty little place, you can tell from the postcards and photos in the magazines. Very historic, too; the first missionaries in New Zealand settled there in the 1820s. I'm sure that someone will be able to show you the Stone Store and the Kemp House while you're there. And, darling, you must admit that it's time you met your cousins. They are, after all, the only other living relatives you have now.' Her mouth trembled, but she went on bravely, 'They want you to be there, Laurel, so you won't need to feel out of place. Not that you would, anyway. You are like your father; you find it easy to talk to people, even strangers.'

At the mention of her father, Laurel knew she was beaten, but she persisted doggedly, 'I need to do some more work on my thesis.'

'You have finished the first draft and need a change before you start fine-tuning it.'

The words came with a built-in sigh that Laurel noted with a sinking heart. Her mother gave her a small, slightly wobbly smile and continued, 'Darling, I wouldn't ask you, but I agree with this Sophie Barrington—I think she must be Aunt Helen's widowed daughter, the one who lives with them at the homestead—anyway, I agree with her; it's time this silly family feud was ended. You are my mother's only descendant; if Aunt Helen is prepared to bury the hatchet, I think we should reciprocate.' Gesturing at her neatly plastered foot she finished wistfully, 'Unfortunately, there's no way I can go, although I'd love to, so it's up to you. Please, darling.'

Laurel tried one last tack. 'If I go, you'll have no one to look after you.'

'Betty Staples is more than happy to come and stay with me over the weekend.'

Another of Laurel's characteristics was her gracious acceptance of defeat when it was inevitable. 'OK,' she said with resignation. 'Heaven knows, I couldn't agree more, family feuds *are* utterly stupid. How many of these new relatives are there?'

Her mother smiled eagerly. 'Your great-aunt Helen and her husband had at least five children, all of whom, I believe, married and have offspring.'

'So there could be scores of them?' Laurel's topaz eyes widened between the thick black screens of her lashes.

'That's not very likely in this day and age of the Pill.' Maureen Webster invested the last word with faint distaste.

Laurel looked up sharply, aware that it was one of the tragedies of her mother's life that she had been able to bear only one child.

Her mother was watching her, following the play of emotion across her daughter's deceptively ingenuous features. With a wan little smile she said, 'Darling, don't go if you really don't want to; I don't want to persuade you to do something you're going to hate. It's just that it would be—nice—to contact them. I've felt so alone since your father died.'

Laurel's heart melted. Her parents had shared a very happy marriage; since her father's death eight months before she had had to watch helplessly as her mother surrendered to a gentle despair, her heart and mind set firmly in the past.

If there was any possibility that these unknown relatives might help her recover her normal hope and resilience, well, a weekend in Kerikeri was a small enough price to pay.

'Of course I'll go,' she said gently, adding, with a glint of humour, 'but you're going to have to tell me *why* Gran and her twin sister vowed not to speak to each other from the age of eighteen until the day they died.'

Her mother looked uncomfortable. 'I don't know all the ramifications; Mother never said anything about it beyond the fact that she had a twin sister in Kerikeri, but I believe it was for the classic reason—a man.'

Laurel's soft, expressive mouth pulled into a moue of distaste.

'Exactly,' her mother said mournfully, 'but they were a tempestuous, stubborn pair.'

'Gran? Tempestuous and stubborn?' Recalling very clearly her grandmother's thin, disciplined face, and her trick of pausing as though she thought every sentence through before speaking, Laurel lifted winged black brows.

Her mother nodded. 'Oh, yes. She learned to control it eventually, but she had a very quick temper. A little like you, in fact. You look alike, too.'

Laurel rolled her eyes. ' "Pocket Venus," ' she said, savagely mimicking the man who, only the night before, had bestowed the hackneyed compliment on her. 'Dear heaven, am I sick of being called that! It's so trite and patronising. Being five feet one is the pits. I'd give anything for legs six inches longer.'

'Then you'd be bewailing the fact that you were short-waisted,' her mother retorted, her habitual air of gentle melancholy lightened by a gleam of humour. 'You're perfectly in proportion, and Venus was beautiful, you know. There are thousands of women who'd envy you that lovely ivory skin and those magnificent eyes, even if they are on a slant.'

'Only my mother could think me beautiful. I'll settle for nice but ordinary. How about the thousands of freckles?' her graceless daughter teased with a grin. 'I can't think of any woman who'd envy me those.'

'They look like a powdering of gold dust,' Mrs Webster told her firmly. 'And there are not thousands, you silly woman, just a few hundreds. *And* if you'd wear a hat when you are outside there wouldn't be any! Anyway, a lot of men find them fascinating. Now, enough of this side-tracking. According to Sophie Barrington, the anniversary celebrations will take the form of a big lunch for family and friends on the Saturday, followed by a party in the evening.' She rustled through the letter in her hand. 'Yes, although Sophie says here that the evening party is really for the young ones. No doubt, at their age, Aunt Helen and her husband tire easily. Then on the Sunday there'll be a church service. They'd like you to be up there for the Friday night, if you can, when there's a small dinner for the immediate family. Sophie says that it would probably be better to meet some of them before you are inflicted with them all on the Saturday! That's thoughtful, isn't it? There's a bed at the homestead for you, or if you prefer she'll book you into a motel.'

'I prefer,' Laurel said quickly, barely repressing a grimace. Far better to stay in the impersonal comfort of a motel room than with relatives she didn't know, relatives with whom she could have absolutely nothing in common. 'What's this about a homestead? Do they live on a station? Are they members of the landed gentry?'

Her voice was lightly mocking, but there was a bitter undertone that made her mother look sharply at her. She bit her lip. Martin had come from a family that prided itself on its wealth, and its standing in the community, although neither wealth nor background had made him anything but a lousy husband. Hastily pushing the corroding memories to the back of her mind, she concentrated on her mother's answer.

'I don't really know.' Mrs Webster's brow wrinkled. 'No, I don't think they can live on a farm. I'm sure I can remember Mother once saying that she grew up on an orchard. I know they had plenty of money.'

'Bottom's dropped out of the kiwi fruit market,' Laurel said knowledgeably, nodding her golden brown head. 'A lot of orchardists pulled out their citrus to plant kiwi fruit, and apparently with the drop in overseas prices many of them are having a hard struggle to survive. Your aunt and her family are probably up to their ears in debt.'

'It's possible, although with old money it's not so likely. Not that it matters. I'll write to Sophie Barrington and tell her that, although I can't come, you will take my place.' Another fugitive gleam of mischief lightened her expression as she noted her daughter's wistful gaze at the magnificent view across the Waitemata Harbour. 'Cheer up, darling, civilisation doesn't end at the harbour bridge, you know.'

'Says who?' Laurel returned inelegantly, as she scrambled to her feet. 'Look, I have to go, I'm meeting Sarah Kirkpatrick for lunch in ten minutes; you do what you think best with that invitation. I must confess, I'm getting rather curious about all these new relatives.' She followed up a kiss on her mother's soft cheek with a hug. 'Who knows? I might find out more about the feud. He must have been some man, whoever he was, to cause trouble that lasted for over sixty years!'

Three weeks later she was waiting in a lay-by at the top of a short steep hill, reviewing a map with all the enthusiasm of a Christian listening to the lions snarl in the arena. Warm spring sunlight beat in through the open car window, bringing with it a faint but delicious fragrance that stirred memories. Laurel's straight nose, with its dusting of freckles, wrinkled as she sought the connection.

Of course! When Laurel was a child her mother's favourite scent had been orange blossom. And that was what she was smelling now, the fragrance of millions of orange flowers on the breeze.

With it came a subtle lifting of her spirits. Perhaps, she thought, ever the optimist, this weekend spent in the house of unknown relatives, honouring the sixtieth wedding anniversary of a great-aunt who had held a grudge for at least that long, wouldn't be so bad at all. Unfortunately, she was going to get to know this forbidding person far more intimately than she wanted to; a motel room had been unobtainable. Apparently, Kerikeri didn't have enough accommodation to hold all the revellers, so she was doomed to be a guest at the homestead.

'Which is,' she muttered, tracing the route into Kerikeri with a short, unpolished nail, 'through the village and down *here*, and then a turn *here*, and—yes, that looks like it. If I go off the tarmac I've gone too far. Right. On your way, Laurel.'

Kerikeri was a bustling little village with a prosperous air in spite of the downturn in the kiwi fruit industry. Perhaps the orange flowers that were scenting the air had saved the orchardists from the dire predictions of the economists. Her wide brow wrinkled in a frown of concentration as Laurel negotiated the roundabout at the entrance to the town and proceeded cautiously down the main street, busy with shoppers.

Almost immediately she made the first of her turns, then wound along a leafy road where bamboo and Japanese cedar hedges hid the orchards from sight. The second turning was obvious; firmly squashing a flock of incipient butterflies in her stomach, she took it, and began to look for a gate on the left with the name Forsythe on it.

It appeared in a massive hedge of lilly pilly trees. Her stomach gave an odd leap as she pulled up and stared through the opening down a drive sheltered by huge trees; jacarandas, some sort of flowering cherry, magnolias . . .

Old money indeed, she thought, shamingly conscious of the fact that her palms were damp on the steering-wheel of her aged but reliable Ford Escort. This place looked like a cross between an English estate and a millionaire's playground on some subtropical island. Whipping out a comb, she tidied the thick wavy hair that helped give her heart-shaped face some substance.

Her small chin jutted in a gesture that substituted apprehension with defiance as she set the car in motion once more. But after about four hundred metres the drive divided into two, and she came once more to a sudden halt. Peering past a huge camphor laurel tree, she thought she could discern a house somewhere along the left fork, so headed off in that direction, only to realise as she came up to it that what she had found was a complex of buildings which, from their size and shape, formed the working part of the orchard.

Halting in a large paved parking area, she gazed around in some dismay. More huge trees, pohutukawas this time, and yes, to one side was what definitely appeared to be a house, but across the wide courtyard was an enormous shed, built in the same style and of the same bricks. Several cars were parked outside it.

She eased the car into the shade of one of the trees, wiped her palms on a handkerchief, then climbed out. It was very still, surprisingly warmer than Auckland had been, and the atmosphere was impregnated with that orange-blossom sweetness, far from subtle now in the golden air. For a moment she stood still, letting the sweet scent and the warmth of the sun soak into her, her gaze appreciative as she surveyed the complex. It had a settled, harmonious air, the buildings gracious in spite of their utilitarian purposes.

A shrill but tuneful whistle from behind the biggest building reminded her of where she was. Setting her mouth firmly she walked across to the front door of the house and rang the bell.

Silence. She rang again, listening with half an ear to the whistled tune, then jumped as the door was flung open.

For some reason she had expected a woman, but there was no doubt about the sex of the person who opened the door, mainly because to her first shocked gaze he appeared to be naked. Tall, over six feet, and built with a rangy symmetry that held the explicit promise of power, he was clad in a pair of shorts, hidden mostly by a towel, and nothing else.

Laurel gulped, her mouth forming the first letter of a man's name, but immediately she realised that this man was not Martin, not the husband she had left barely two years ago.

That first, appalled glance had caught the similarities, mainly of size and colouring, but with the second glance she noted the differences. Her shocked gaze flicked up the length of powerfully moulded thighs to rest for a timeless second on a lean flat stomach, and from thence to the intriguing scrolls of hair on the broad tanned chest, her eyes widening helplessly to take in the wide shoulders and taut midriff. A golden brown man whose sleekly outlined musculature was emphasised by a haze of damp, crisply curling hair, he possessed an elemental attraction that made something she had thought long dead stretch lazily deep within her and wake to laughing, malicious life.

Overwhelmed, her eyes flashed to the hard-planed angles of his face, and were held pinned by a cold blue stare from between dark lashes that blatantly contrasted with hair the colour of dark honey.

No, this man didn't look in the least like Martin, who had been as handsome as a Greek god. This man didn't look as though weakness was a word he admitted into his vocabulary, and she had discovered that Martin's classical features hid a whole series of very glaring weaknesses.

Unconsciously, she took a step backwards. Above the mantelpiece in her mother's house was a Spanish officer's sword, exquisitely hilted, but the business end of it was all sharp ferocity, a blade of the finest steel. The heavy-lidded eyes that were watching her with such unsettling intensity were the exact blue of that sheen, and every bit as dangerous as the blade.

Her breath stopped in her chest; she felt the first unwanted stab of attraction, sharp and painful, bitter as gall. All the pretty apricot colour drained from her cheeks, allowing the small freckles to stand out like tiny gold coins across her nose. Through the scramble of thoughts colliding in her brain, she realised that this was a man who would never be overlooked.

A Maori proverb popped into her mind. 'E kore te tino tangata e ngaro i roto i te tokomaha.' A chief cannot be lost in a crowd.

Unable to tear her gaze away, she saw his lashes droop, hiding the forbidding glitter that had kept her spellbound. The towel was flung over one strong tanned shoulder. His brows snapped together; with an unsmiling look he demanded curtly, 'Yes?'

Laurel's mouth was dry. Swallowing, she had to suffer the way his gaze pinpointed the small betraying movement as she responded too quickly, 'Is this the Forsythe homestead?'

'No. You've taken the wrong turning, this is the manager's house.' His voice was deep, curiously harsh, yet it stirred something inside her.

Desperate to get away with as much of her dignity intact as she could, she said in her coolest tone, 'I see, thank you, I'll go back and——'

'Is your business necessary?' The words resounded in her ears, but didn't make sense. When she stared at him in bewilderment he elaborated with a crispness that barely hid his irritation, 'They're rather busy at the homestead today.'

'Yes,' she said inanely. 'That's why I'm here. There, I mean.'

What on earth was the matter with her? She had seen better-looking men than this before—although rarely in so few clothes—but she was no blushing *ingénue* to be set on her beam-ends by a half-naked man, even one who was stamped with such potent masculine authority.

But of course she knew why she couldn't look away. Self-contempt lashed her with its vicious whips; she went even paler, but her eyes continued to cling to his.

He was still frowning, his gaze roving her form with an absorption that would have been insolent if it hadn't so clearly been unconscious. 'Who are you, then?'

She should have asked whether her identity was the manager's business, but although she bridled at his arrogance she answered without hesitation, 'I'm Laurel Webster.'

'Webster?' The black brows drew together, then sudden illumination lit his hard face with comprehension. 'Webster? Great-Aunt Laura's daughter? No, you'd have to be a granddaughter, surely.'

'Yes. Who are you?'

A smile that held little humour but considerable wolfish anticipation lit his face. 'I am your second cousin,' he said with smooth satisfaction. 'Or your first cousin once removed, perhaps. Sophie would know the correct relationship. Alick Forsythe. Helen Forsythe's grandson.'

'But I thought——' At his enquiring look she blushed, but went on sturdily, 'I thought you said that this was the manager's house.'

'It is.' Those amazing eyes lingered over her features, something hard and dismissive gleaming in their depths like a diamond set in steel. 'I manage the place and live here. My widowed aunt, Sophie, who invited you, lives with her parents at the homestead.'

'Which is back down the other fork in the road,' she said, eager to get away. 'I'll——'

He smiled sardonically, interrupting with careless authority, 'Exactly. If you wait for a few minutes I'll get into some clothes and come with you.'

It was a kind thought, so why did she suspect his motives?

For the same reason that she was behaving like a refugee from a slapstick movie, she thought with sick despair. Hadn't she learned her lesson? But he was clearly waiting for an answer, so before she had time to change her mind she said, 'Yes.' And because it seemed too bald a reply she added lamely, 'Thank you.'

'Good.' His smile was incredible; it sizzled with charm and something else she had never encountered before: a kind of insolent appreciation that set up little pulses of sensation right throughout her body. 'Come on in,' he invited. 'I'll be about five minutes.'

He led her to a big room that looked out on to a wide terrace draped with jasmine, and a swimming-pool, and thence over a lawn to a thick border of shrubs and trees.

'Won't be a minute,' he said and took himself through a door.

Laurel was horrified to hear her breath ease out as though she had been holding it ever since he had appeared in front of her. He was, she thought wearily, absolutely bloody gorgeous, which was odd because he certainly wasn't handsome. In fact, his features were too harsh for masculine beauty, his mouth arrogant and inflexible, although his bottom lip was interestingly full. And his eyes were strangely detached, the heavy lids giving him a sleepy appearance that was belied by their keen scrutiny.

Uneasily, she walked across the lovely, cool room to the heavy glass doors, her abstracted glance roaming to

a shady bower at the other end of the house. There the
pergola over the terrace peaked; beneath it, the floor
dropped down into wide steps, forming a square seating
area around a table. Dark green cushions padded the
steps. Beyond, adding a slow musical tinkle to the sweet
air, was a tiny waterfall over a ledge of rocks.

The sun caught something on a rocky ledge, but she
couldn't see what it was that crouched there behind the
water, merely that it was a sleek and gleaming green.

She stood for a long moment staring, her mind ines-
capably drifting back to Alick Forsythe. As well as that
splendid physical presence, she had discerned a hard intelligence in those amazing eyes. But then, she thought
with a derisory movement of her mouth, she had been
sure she had seen intelligence in Martin, too. And she
had been wrong. Martin had resented the fact that she
was 'clever'.

Intelligence was important to Laurel. Wincing, she
turned back into the room. She could still hear the sneer
in Martin's voice when he said the word, the sneer that
had quickly become full-blown contempt. That shat-
tering episode of her life, the year of her marriage, had
started with the same mindless attraction she felt now,
an enslavement to the purely physical.

That was *her* weakness, a fatal flaw. She had looked
at Martin and wanted him, capitulated completely to his
intense sexual attraction.

Her soft mouth tightened as she recalled the pain and
humiliation that had followed that initial stupidity.
Blankly, she looked down at a beautiful Persian carpet,
barely recognising the glowing colours and intricate,
stylised pattern, her mouth thin with bitter irony.

Never again. The year she had spent in hell had made
her so deeply suspicious of desire that she had vowed
never to fall beneath its spell again. And she thought
she had managed to repress it, until she had looked
through an open door and seen a man bearing a strong

superficial resemblance to the husband who had stripped her confidence from her with petulant cruelty.

Not that they really looked so much alike, Martin and Alick Forsythe, although they were roughly the same height and build and colouring. Instead of that unusual blue, Martin's eyes had been a wicked green and he was more slightly built than Alick. But they both had the same golden skin and the same insolent animal magnetism.

However Alick, this new-found cousin, looked to be a much tougher character, his self-assurance based on an inner confidence that Martin had only aspired to, envying as he did those who had it with a sour rancour.

But then, how good a judge of personality was she? She had thought that Martin had loved her, that he had had it in him to be a tender man, a good husband and father, and she had been proved wrong. Perhaps she was wrong about Alick, too. Perhaps, beneath that splendidly self-sufficient authority, he was as small and as mean as Martin had proved to be, so lacking in courage that he had needed to beat her spirit into submission to bolster his own.

The abrupt summons of the telephone jerked her back from her gloomy memories. She waited, thinking that perhaps there might be a connection in the bedroom for Alick Forsythe to answer, but after another three rings she realised that she was going to have to deal with it.

Halfway across the room she sighed with relief when the ringing died, only to feel infinitely more uncomfortable at the coo of a feminine voice on the answerphone system.

'Alick,' it said, 'I'm not going to be able to get home until late tonight; Derek's just told us that the staff meeting is going to last longer than normal. Sorry. It *would* have to be tonight, wouldn't it? Would you mind very much making my apologies to everyone? I shouldn't be too much later than seven.' The voice deepened into caressing intimacy. 'Love you lots, darling.'

Laurel bit her lip, and laughed at herself. Well, of course a man of Alick Forsythe's age, the early thirties, would be married. Men with that natural charisma didn't stay single for long. Probably he had several kids at school, she decided, conscious of a sweet relief flooding through her.

He was fully dressed when he returned, the fitting trousers and cotton shirt emphasising his lean strongly muscled body, the restrained earthy beige of the material paradoxically brightening the colour of those amazing eyes.

Above the stupid thudding of her heart, Laurel said, 'Your wife rang to say she wouldn't be home until seven. I'm sorry, I didn't realise you had an answerphone, so I heard her message.'

'You're a bit premature,' he said calmly, watching her with amused comprehension. 'Jenna and I aren't getting married until January.'

'Congratulations,' she said, smiling up at him, much more confident now because he was safe. 'A summer wedding is always nice.' Mortification at her inanity cut the babbling short.

Those steel-blue eyes were fixed on her wedding finger. 'Is that when you were married?'

She still wore her ring. It helped ward off too-susceptible undergraduates. And perhaps it acted as a warning not to get carried away by a handsome face and a blazing sexual attraction. 'No,' she said quietly. 'I was married in the autumn. But my husband is dead.'

'I'm sorry,' he said, and he sounded it.

She shrugged, knowing that she should explain that the marriage had died even before she left Martin, knowing that she wouldn't. 'It was a tragedy. I'm over it now.'

In some ways. In others, she would never recover.

'You must have been a baby when you married him.'

She grimaced. 'Yes. Only twenty.'

So young, and so completely, innocently, naïve. Blinded by her first experience of passion, convinced that this was going to last all her life, she had insisted on marrying Martin. He had wanted it too; later she realised that he believed that marriage would make her his possession. And her mother, perhaps foolishly sentimental, had persuaded her husband that Laurel was old enough to know her own mind.

'So how old are you now?' he asked as he opened the door into the hall.

'Twenty-three.'

She felt his searching sideways perusal as he said, on an amused note, 'You look about fifteen.'

'I know,' she said gloomily. 'You have no idea how hard it is to achieve credibility with students.'

The sunlight outside was dazzling, so strong that she couldn't see anything for a few seconds.

'Students?' he asked in that deep, slightly grating voice, locking the door behind him. 'You're a teacher?'

Like his Jenna. 'I suppose you could call me that. I'm a junior lecturer at university.' His laughter was free and unforced. She grinned. 'Yes, I know.'

'I imagine you have the greatest difficulty fending off all those earnest young men.'

Faint colour tinged her cheeks. 'Well, it happens, but mostly I have trouble convincing them that I know what I'm talking about.'

He opened the car door and ushered her into it, then swung around the front to the passenger's seat. Pretending not to watch him, Laurel told herself fervently that she was glad he was safely engaged, otherwise he would be altogether too disturbing. It seemed that, somewhere in her subconscious, she was fixated on lean rangy men who walked with a predatory supple grace.

But she was older now, older and wiser, the fresh innocence of youth tarnished by experience, no longer at the mercy of an impressionable heart and her hormones. And Alick was engaged to the woman with the soft, pretty voice, so Laurel was in no danger from him at all.

'And what,' he enquired as he folded his long legs beneath the dash, 'do you talk about?'

'History.'

'You're an MA student?'

'Yes,' she admitted.

'Writing a thesis? On what?'

She chuckled as she set the car in motion. 'I don't suppose you'd believe that it's on the theory that until a couple of hundred years ago every important decision made in humanity's history had, for at least one of the protagonists, someone who was suffering from toothache?'

He grinned, his expression relaxing into an immensely attractive humour. 'No, I don't really think I would believe that. It's a fascinating theory, and may well be true, but I'd have to point out that the evidence might be a little difficult to arrive at.'

'That's what my supervisor said too. So I'm doing a history of the Kauri Milling Company, one of the big firms that laid waste to the kauri forests in the last century and the beginning of this, when everyone thought the trees would go on forever.'

'Turn left here,' he said absently, as they came to the fork in the road. 'Are you enjoying it?'

'Yes; the research is fascinating and I think it's shaping up quite well.'

She drove with extreme care between more magnificent trees and wide lawns towards a large white house of the sort that had been fashionable in the early part of the century. Double-storeyed, it faced the drive, with several steps up to a wide entrance porch backed by panelled double doors, set in long glass windows. An interesting mixture of herbaceous borders and subtropical lushness surrounded the house with colour and form, and around the corner french windows opened out from the interior on to a shady terrace. It was serene and graciously mature in its setting, a far cry from the stained wood and dark brick modernity of the manager's complex.

'Is this where my grandmother lived before she left home?' Laurel asked a little stiffly. It appeared that, like Martin's family, this branch of the Forsythes was stinking rich. All her defensiveness came clanging back.

'Left home? Well, I suppose you could call it that. On the day before her sister's wedding she ran away with the man her sister was engaged to marry.'

'What?' She turned a horrified look at him. 'And your grandmother—that sister—wants me at this celebration?'

'I imagine,' he said calmly as she switched off the engine, 'that she considers the feud has outlived itself. Your grandparents are long dead and Gran is very family-minded.'

He spoke with unemotional detachment but her swift surprised glance caught a fleeting gentleness in his hard-hewn features. He loved his grandmother.

For some reason this put her at a disadvantage. She found she didn't want to think of Alick Forsythe as being capable of tenderness. Touching her dry lips with the tip of her tongue, she asked wryly, 'She does know I'm coming, doesn't she?'

He nodded, looking cynical and amused at the same time. 'Yes, she asked for you and your mother to be invited. It surprised all of us, but we pander to her now.'

The sun was now low enough in the sky to line his profile with a fierce gold. Laurel stared straight ahead but even when she closed her eyes she could see that inflexible outline; bold, fleshless, an arrogant silhouette from the straight forehead to the clean, jutting lines of his jaw and chin. And the stark, beautifully moulded curve of his lips, a stunning contrast to the forceful angles and planes. Not a hint of softness or slackness anywhere. She sensed that he could be just as ruthless as that profile.

Antagonism flooded her being, sharp and hot and resentful, but in spite of it her body ached with a forbidden hunger. Why, oh, why was she such a fool? She had been that way before and been burned by it.

Forewarned was definitely forearmed, but the existence of his Jenna was an even better shield against her own foolishness. Laurel didn't poach.

He was so tall that she felt very small and insignificant as she walked beside him up the steps and into the foyer, a large room panelled halfway up to the ceiling with warm golden kauri, a fireplace filled with greenery in the centre, and behind it a magnificent suspended staircase of the same timber. Two large modern sofas looked as well used as the fireplace. The afternoon sun glowed through a heraldic window above the huge doors.

'The Forsythe crest,' Alick told her when he saw her eyes come to rest on it. 'Gran had it put in as a Christmas present after she and Grandy were married.'

Something moved in the pit of her stomach. She felt totally alone, almost intimidated, but hid it by feigning interest, gazing about with lowered lashes. The serene formality of the furnishings suited the house and the garden. Laurel thought of her flippant suggestion that the Forsythes might be suffering from a cashflow problem, and made a small hidden grimace.

Alick gave her a cool, almost taunting smile, before calling, 'Are you receiving, Gran?'

'Of course I'm receiving,' a voice answered, so like her grandmother's crisp tones that Laurel's eyes darkened for a moment to shadows.

'Good, because Laurel Webster is here.' He urged her along the passage to the right of the stairs, stopping to hold the door open, watching her with an indifference that felt like a betrayal.

Her first step into the room revealed that her very worst suspicions were only too validated. Physically, Helen Forsythe was almost identical to the twin sister who had died five years ago, from the white hair to the thin lined face and surprisingly firm lips. Both had the tilted topaz eyes that Laurel had inherited, both the creamy skin and the long aristocratic fingers, now a little twisted by arthritis.

Laurel stood stock-still in the doorway, her expression revealing her shock and dismay. When Alick's hand closed on her forearm she had to pull herself away, because the temptation to relax against his lean strength almost overpowered her.

'Well, we were identical twins,' her great-aunt snapped, instantly divining the cause of her stillness and pallor. 'Come on in, girl, and try not to look as though you've seen a ghost.'

'I'm sorry,' Laurel said after a taut, humming moment when, to her horror, she thought she might faint.

Her great-aunt subjected her to an open survey. 'You look like us too, although you're a little taller. We were known as "the pocket Venuses".'

Laurel groaned. Miffed, Helen Forsythe said, 'It was a compliment!'

'Don't you believe it,' Laurel told her drily. 'It was a put-down.'

The older woman suddenly smiled. 'Come in and sit down. You look as though you could do with a cup of something. Or something stronger. *I* certainly could. It's not very often that you see yourself as you were sixty years ago walk in through the door. Alick, get us all a glass of sherry, will you?'

So the autocratic old voice could soften, and the smile lose its astringent flavour! Clearly Alick Forsythe was his grandmother's darling.

Like him, she was observant. The faded gold-brown gaze fixed on to the wedding-ring on Laurel's hand. 'You are married?'

'No, no longer.'

Alick's deep voice covered the tense little silence. 'Her husband is dead,' he said.

The shrewd eyes scanned her face. 'You're very young to be widowed,' Helen Forsythe said non-comittally.

Laurel nodded, shielding her thoughts with her lashes, unable to think of anything to say.

'And how is your mother?'

'Furious,' Laurel told her lightly. 'She'd have loved to have come, but, as she told you in her answer, she broke her ankle and still has to stay off it. I have a letter for you from her.'

Alick had gone across to a tray on which stood a crystal decanter of sherry, and some glasses. He gave his grandmother one and brought the second across to Laurel, smiling at her with sympathetic if amused comprehension as she accepted it gratefully. Not normally a sherry drinker, she felt the need for some sort of reviver.

'Are you going to be on time for dinner tonight?' his grandmother asked him, after she had sampled her drink.

'Of course I am,' he assured her, taking his own glass across to the mantelpiece. 'I do try to be on time, you know that.'

Helen Forsythe snorted. 'Yes, but you're late more often than not. There's always something you have to deal with. And Jenna?'

'Unfortunately she's going to be delayed by a staff meeting, but she hopes to be here by seven.'

Something outside caught his attention; in one smooth movement he strode across to the open french window, saying calmly, 'Excuse me, I'll be back in a moment.'

His grandmother said briskly, 'The girl he's engaged to is an assistant primary school teacher. A nice girl. They plan to marry after Christmas.'

Something in her voice made Laurel flinch. Had she seen the way Laurel's eyes had followed him across the room, irresistibly drawn to him? Possibly. Laurel doubted whether those shrewd eyes missed much. 'A summer wedding is lovely,' she said quietly. 'Will you have it in the garden?'

'I think so.' She dismissed the subject, although Laurel was convinced she'd have no hesitation in referring to it again if she thought it would serve a purpose, like once more underlining the fact that Alick was spoken for.

Embarrassed and uneasy, Laurel looked around for a fresh topic of conversation, but before she could come up with one the older woman asked, 'Tell me, was your grandmother happy?'

'You could,' Laurel returned with spirit, 'have asked her yourself, if you'd really wanted to know.'

Helen Forsythe gave a grim smile. 'I, madam, would have stopped this stupid feud years ago, but Laura wouldn't have it. She was always stubborn, cutting off her nose to spite her face more often than not.'

'But she was——' Laurel stopped precipitately.

'Yes, she was the one in the wrong, she stole the man I was going to marry. So she wouldn't meet me again. Pride, I suppose, and shame. Don't look so disbelieving! I forgave her when I realised that I had never really loved John; when I met Hugh, I knew it. Why should I keep up a stupid feud when I was happy?'

Put like that, it seemed logical. Laurel said quietly, 'Whereas she, as I suppose you know, was not at all happy.'

'No, of course I didn't know. She cut herself off from all of us, refused even to keep in contact with our friends. Why wasn't she happy?'

'Perhaps because she always wondered whether Grandfather really did love her. I don't know; I do know that once she said to me, "Make sure that you know what you are doing when you marry; so much hinges on it. And, once it's done, there's no going back."'

'And did you think of that when you got married?'

A sardonic little smile hardened Laurel's mouth. 'Does youth ever listen to wisdom?'

'Rarely, in my experience.' The sound of a car drawing up outside the house turned her white head. 'This will

be my husband and my daughter,' she said. 'Sophie will
show you to your room. I hope you have a happy
weekend with us, Laurel.'

'I'm sure I shall,' she said formally, adding with a
different sort of smile altogether, 'Great-Aunt Helen.'

Almost immediately Sophie Barrington came in
through the door, a tall woman very like the man with
her, her father. One glance at him revealed from whom
Alick Forsythe had inherited those commanding features and the tall rangy body, although the air of blazing
authority and the sleek animal grace were the younger
man's alone. As she was made welcome, Laurel decided
that Hugh Forsythe must always have been gentler, more
amiable, than his grandson. The arrogance, she decided, transferring her thoughtful gaze to her great-aunt's
face, came from their side of the family!

'Where is Alick?' Hugh asked after the babble of
greetings had died down, smiling at his wife with such
affection that it brought a tightness to Laurel's throat.

'He disappeared outside—I gather he saw something
that displeased him.'

'I find that hard to believe,' Sophie commented with
comical emphasis. 'All of the women who work here
adore him; they spend all their time trying to catch his
eye! And the men are too much in awe of him to ma-
linger. Laurel, why don't I show you to your room? You
must be dying to freshen up, and we'll have a cup of tea
in half an hour or so. How does that sound?'

'Blissful,' Laurel told her, smiling gratefully.

The rest of the house was every bit as impressive as
the part she had already seen. Almost mansion size, the
rooms stretched away down corridors that were not in
the least institutional, decorated as they were by the
treasures of several generations with excellent taste and
the money to indulge it. Laurel's cynical eyes surveyed
a tall grandfather clock, mellow with the polish of years,
so old that there was only one hand on its face, then

moved on to a magnificent painting that seemed to bear all the hallmarks of a Turner.

Martin's home, a big station house in the central North Island, had had this air of settled wealth. Yet this house had none of the superficial glitter that had made Martin's home so out of place in its country setting. The Forsythes lived in a house that was unpretentious, yet overwhelming.

'Turner was a friend of the family. It's one of his good ones, isn't it?' Sophie said, opening a door. 'Apparently it was painted from the terrace of the house that Father's grandfather emigrated from. Family tradition has it that the servants took it in turn to hold an umbrella over him while he was sketching, because our great-great-grandmother was sure he'd catch his death of cold. Turner himself didn't seem to worry about his health, did he? All that tying himself to the mast in storms, and hanging out of railway carriages for his art! Now, here we are. There's a bathroom across here, which you'll have to share, I'm afraid, but only with one person, and she's not coming until tomorrow. Do ask if there's anything you need, won't you?'

Left alone, Laurel took a deep breath and looked around the smallish but exceptionally pretty room. Clearly it had once been a child's bedroom, and the white iron bedstead and old pine dressing-table still held some suggestion of the nursery, but the white embroidered spread was a beautiful piece of work that no child would be allowed near, and the bowls of flowers were charmingly cottagey in a sophisticated manner; as was the selection of old silver on the dressing-table, and the powerful water-colour of a coastal scene on the wall. Laurel's eyes were caught and held by it. It looked serene, as beautiful as any northern bay in summer, but behind the glamour of sparkling water and pristine sands was the dark shadow of night. For all the tranquillity, one was very aware that in winter that same sea would smash with elemental force upon those sands.

An odd little shudder moved like a trickle of ice down Laurel's spine. Shrugging, she walked across to look out over the gardens and the smooth sweep of the lawns to a block of land between high shelter belts, cross-hatched by rows upon rows of citrus trees, small and round, the dark green foliage almost covered by the brilliant orange globes of fruit.

People were picking those fruit into big canvas bags around their waists. Leaning out a little, she heard laughter, and was just in time to see a man she recognised as Alick leave the group and make his way back to the house. The sun struck flames of dark amber from his hair and picked out the slashing features, the strong nose and chin, and broad, sweeping cheekbones.

Something stirred in her stomach, releasing a flood of aching sweetness through her. Desire, she thought, disgusted with herself yet unable to control the honeyed sensations.

The simple reaction of female to male; the sleazy joke that made her want men who had little to recommend them but a certain pantherish stride, a lean muscular body with certain proportions of leg to torso, shoulder to narrow hips; men with golden skin and tawny hair.

It had propelled her into a marriage where not even lust had been able to make lovemaking anything but a disappointment; unable to be aroused by Martin in any but the most basic way, after a while she hadn't been able to respond to him at all.

And she had disappointed him just as much. Her lips tightened as she watched her cousin stride smoothly across the brilliant grass of spring. Learn by your mistakes, she adjured herself fiercely. And remember Jenna.

As though her unspoken thoughts had reached him, he stopped and lifted his head, his eyes roving across the upper storey until he found her. She would have liked to withdraw, but it would have been far too obvious. Instead she leaned forward and called, 'What are they picking?'

'Tangeloes,' he told her. 'Like to come down and see?'

The sun glowed on his face. That feral turbulence thundered through her body. She smiled back. 'Another time, if I may? Your aunt has promised me a cup of tea.'

His teeth showed white and faintly cruel in the shadowed skin of his face as he grinned. She despised herself for feeling weak at the thought of them touching her fainting flesh, savage but gentle in the kind of love-bites she had only ever imagined.

How can you be turned on by teeth? she asked herself bitterly as she turned away, knowing even as she tried to reduce her emotions to parody that it wasn't working.

It took an effort, but she pushed him from her mind and went to wash and change into a thin knit dress in pale peach, one of her favourite outfits in spite of the fact that the warm colour emphasised her freckles.

CHAPTER TWO

DOWNSTAIRS again, Laurel found the Forsythes gathered around a massive silver tea-service from which Sophie was pouring for them all, scolding gently as she did so.

'...in the middle of the day,' she finished, as Laurel came in.

Alick smiled down at her. 'Darling Aunt, four o'clock is not the middle of the day!'

Although visibly melting, she continued sternly, 'Mother is not supposed to drink sherry at all, so don't quibble about the time, Alick, and don't think you can get around me with that smile! You don't have to deal with the aftermath!'

'There'll be no aftermath,' her mother said indignantly, as Laurel came across another superb Persian carpet, bigger but not more beautiful than the one in Alick's sitting-room. 'Ah, there you are, Laurel! Fully recovered from your drive up?'

'Yes, thank you.' I will not look at him, she had promised herself as she had come down the stairs, but she couldn't resist a fleeting glance as she smiled with studied impartiality around the room. He was looking somewhat sardonic, blue eyes narrowed, the debatable mouth with its sensual lower lip tightly reined in.

'Have some tea,' her aunt said hospitably. 'Alick, dear, pull that table a little closer to the chair, will you? Thank you. There, now sit down, Laurel, and tell us all about yourself.'

It was the sort of command that normally made Laurel shrink, but she managed to retain her composure as she gave them a quick run-through of her life up until then, only briefly touching on the tragedies, highlighting the happy events, barely touching on her marriage.

32

'To lose your husband and your father, as well as your grandmother, within such a short time! So sad,' Aunt Sophie sighed, her pleasant face compassionate.

Laurel bit her lip. She would have to tell them. In a cool little voice she said, 'My husband and I were separated when he was killed.'

Apparently this was almost as bad. The older woman's aristocratic face registered shock and then commiseration. 'Oh, I am sorry, Laurel,' she said. 'What a pity! It's a such a shame, a marriage break-down, isn't it? So—so bad for the self-esteem! And now you are catching up on your studies. When will we know when your thesis has been accepted? Or passed? What *does* happen to theses? Alick, you did one; why didn't you tell me what happens to them so that I wouldn't be making a fool of myself right now?'

Everyone smiled, and Alick defused, with smooth worldliness, what could have been a rather tense moment. It was all very low-key, and, in spite of the fact that they were all deliberately making things easy for her, Laurel relaxed. This kind of social interaction she could cope with; her mother was excellent at it, the technique well understood, practised to perfection over many years.

She discovered that tonight was going to be a small dinner, but that all of the extended family would be there for lunch the following day, including a vast number of Great-Uncle Hugh's relatives, more than a few of whom had travelled from overseas for the occasion.

'We are scattered the length and breadth of the country,' he told her in his dry courteous manner. 'Most of us are farming folk, but there are some townspeople among us. Few, however, manage to straddle the line as successfully as Alick does.'

Her surprise must have been obvious, for he elaborated with quiet pride, 'He runs the family holdings, so he has an apartment in Auckland as well as one in San Francisco. He chooses to spend as much time as he can here, where he was born and brought up, but, alas, we don't see as much of him as we would like to.'

Laurel's interest in the circumstances of Alick's birth and upbringing must have shown in her too-easily-read features, for Uncle Hugh, as he had suggested she call him, went on, 'His mother was a delightful woman, very artistic, but she needed more than we could give her here, so when Alick was three she left him and his father and went off to England. She's very happy there now, and has made a good name for herself as a concert violinist. And when John, Alick's father, died a few years ago Alick took over from him. Which means we don't see nearly enough of him, alas. In spite of the technical advances which we are assured are making our lives much easier, Alick seems to work harder and harder, doesn't he, Sophie?'

'Yes, poor Jenna misses him badly,' Sophie chimed in with a sigh. 'Of course, she works hard too. It's a very responsible job, hers, and she's very good at it, the dear girl. The little children love her, and she's so sweet with them. You'll like her, Laurel, I'm sure. She's a darling.'

Laurel smiled and made some appropriate response, wishing they would get on to some other topic, relaxing when they did and she could wonder just how his mother's departure from his life when he was three had affected Alick Forsythe.

It must have helped to put some of the hardness into his expression, she thought, covertly studying him. And perhaps the maverick artistic gene had given him that air of compelling, dangerous magnetism. It might even have given him the subtle, searching intelligence she was admiring as he talked with his grandmother about a book they had both read recently. So he had achieved a Master's degree; as his deep voice resounded in her ears, she was no longer surprised. She even felt shame that she had wanted to dismiss him as an intellectual lightweight, like Martin. It had been an instinctive defence mechanism, but it had been petty.

Alick Forsythe was nothing like the man she had married.

Her heart ached for the small boy whose mother had deserted him. However loving his father and grandparents had been, there must have been nights when he had cried himself to sleep, longing for his mother.

She looked away, far too fascinated by the play of expression over those hard-honed features, and with determination entered into a conversation with Sophie about the tourist attractions in both Kerikeri and the Bay of Islands.

Then it was time to change for dinner; she chose a simple silk dress her mother had bought her several years ago, a light soft swirl in a gold the colour of Jersey cream, made up her face with a little more than her usual care, and slipped thin hoops of gold in her ears and a narrow gold bracelet on her wrist.

Would she be suitably dressed? Would Jenna outshine her by too much?

But Jenna was quite different from the super-smooth beauty she had imagined. With superb skin set off by luxuriantly curly hair of a pale soft brown that emphasised tender blue eyes, of course she had to be tall and slender, making Laurel feel like a dumpy midget. And she was young; only nineteen or so, Laurel guessed, which would make Alick at least twelve years older than she. Pretty in a fresh, open way, she was patently in love with the man she was engaged to, her soft eyes dazzled, almost awed, when they dwelt on his face. She smiled at Laurel with a warm friendliness that should have set her at ease, but Laurel was horrified to feel the cold barb of jealousy in her heart.

Appalled at the primitive strength of her emotions and very aware of Alick's steel-blue eyes resting on her too often, she set out to be as charming as she could. Another cousin was there, Sophie's sister Faith Carey, with her husband Jack, a tall couple who lived in Hawke Bay, that dry, hot province on the south-east coast of the North Island. From a few stray comments Laurel discovered that they owned a large chunk of the province's hill country. One of their daughters had just flown in from a finishing school in Switzerland to be at the anniversary, and was driving up with her doctor sister early the following morning.

Laurel's brows must have climbed a bit at this nugget of information, for across the table she saw Jenna hide a smile, and after dinner the younger woman confided, 'I know how you feel, I was startled too when I first realised just how wealthy the Forsythes are. They don't act as though they've got lots of money, do they? I mean, you'd never know from looking at them.'

Laurel allowed herself a swift survey of the other people in the room. Was Jenna quite as artless as her remarks indicated? It was possible that she mightn't recognise expensive English tailoring or a Dior dress, probably bought some years ago but still timelessly elegant on Faith Carey's slim figure. But surely she'd realise that the superb pearls around Sophie's neck were not fakes, nor the exquisite but far from flashy diamond ring matched to the earrings. Certainly these people were not flamboyant or obvious, but they had an enviable air of assurance that could only come from a secure, well-established background.

Smiling, she said, 'Old money likes to be inconspicuous, so I've heard.'

'But you're one of them.' Jenna's bright eyes moved over her. 'I mean, a part of the family. You've got the look.'

'The look?' With the best will in the world Laurel couldn't hide her puzzlement.

Jenna was gazing earnestly at her. 'Like Alick. Sort of—imperious, in a nice kind of way. But of course you are cousins, so it would be a little odd if there weren't some resemblance. Not physically—there, you couldn't

be more different—but there's an air about you all.
Confident.'

A thin wash of pale apricot heated Laurel's cheeks.
She hid it by nodding, at last aware of what the younger
woman was doing. Jenna must have picked up something of the tingling pull she felt for Alick and was dis-
tancing her by grouping them together as family.

Was it so obvious, that bitter, reluctant attraction? A
mixture of shame and embarrassment led to her saying
a little too heartily, 'Oh, do you think so?'

Jenna smiled, patting a lock of glossy hair into place.
'Oh, it's there, although it's hard to pinpoint. But family
resemblances usually are, aren't they? I mean, I have
some cousins who really look like both sides of the
family, although neither side looks like the other, surprisingly enough.'

She was not exactly boring; it was just that she was
trying very hard, and she seemed very young. With the
firmness of experience, Laurel corralled a tiny yawn and
listened with a small smile to a string of artless confi-
dences, glad when they at last came to end with the observation, 'Alick told me that you're going to be a teacher
too.'

'Now how did he get that idea?' Genuinely puzzled,
Laurel looked across the room to where her cousin, his
long-limbed body disposed against the mantelpiece in an
attitude which, she suspected, was atypically relaxed, was
smiling with cool charm down at his aunt Faith. As
though her glance were tangible, he looked up, and
something flashed from his narrowed eyes.

His lashes cut it off immediately, but it shook Laurel
to her heart's core.

Oh, *God*, she thought, as she dragged her attention
back to Jenna, even managing a sunny smile as the
younger woman explained, '...that you were doing a
history degree, so I just assumed that you were planning
to teach.'

'No,' Laurel said evenly. 'I think I'd be the worst teacher you could ever come across. I have little patience and probably no discipline.'

'Oh, discipline is quite easy,' Jenna informed her with a hint of smugness. 'I have no problems because I mean what I say, and I truly like children. They sense these things, don't they?'

Laurel had had very little to do with children since being one herself, but she nodded and tried to look interested as Jenna gave her a few examples of her dealings with children, finishing with a further question about Laurel's plans.

A little reluctantly, she admitted, 'I don't know what I'm going to do, beyond the fact that after I've finished my thesis an organisation in Auckland wants me to write the history of a building they've just bought for their headquarters, and then a county council in the centre of the North Island has a mass of historical documents they want reduced to order and published. They can't pay much, but it might be interesting to do.'

Jenna looked at her with some perplexity. 'It sounds fascinating,' she said politely, although it wasn't difficult to discern the doubt in her voice. 'I'm afraid I like the stability of a regular job, but then I've always been conventional.'

Conventional? Ah, well, living with the man one was engaged to probably *was* considered the conventional thing to do nowadays!

For no apparent reason the evening dragged from then on. She was, Laurel decided, more tired than she had realised. No doubt it was the long trip up from Auckland, although three and a half hours couldn't exactly be termed a mammoth journey.

With a strong infusion of will-power, she smiled and responded to these unknown relatives, a little amused at how different their lives had been from hers. Not that she had been brought up in poverty, but, although her father had earned a good salary, he wouldn't have been able to foot it with this lot. Definitely another family from New Zealand's equivalent of the aristocracy, she thought with a wry cynicism that dimmed the glowing amber of her eyes. She seemed doomed to be tangled up with the 'gentry', somehow.

These Forsythes were not like Martin's family, though, most of whom had been aloof and snobbish, a background of breeding and money almost their sole criterion of worth. Her eyes drifted from face to pleasant face, before inevitably coming to rest on the enigmatic countenance of her cousin.

Now, why enigmatic? On the surface of it he seemed to be enjoying himself, his striking, unhandsome face relaxed as he spoke to his uncle. And certainly no one else seemed to sense what was so obvious to her, the tight control, a watchful restrained impatience held in place by an iron will.

A swift glance around the room revealed one person who was not fooled, perhaps. His grandmother was watching him, her expression impassive; as Laurel scanned her face, she transferred her gaze to Jenna, and then quickly across to Laurel herself, and there was a rapidly hidden question there as though Helen Forsythe had seen something she expected, something she recognised, something that worried her.

But so swiftly was the moment gone that Laurel began to wonder if it had meant anything at all. Without missing a cue, her great-aunt rejoined the conversation, and, although Laurel found herself searching the lined, arrogant old countenance, there was no hint of worry or concern in it. To all intents, Helen Forsythe was enjoying herself very much, and hadn't a care in the world beyond hoping for fine weather the next day.

They went to bed early, but Laurel couldn't sleep. Gripped by an intolerable restlessness, she finally padded barefoot out of her room, hoping to find a book to read. After dinner Sophie had given her a quick tour of the main rooms on the ground floor, taking her from the

formal dining-room off the foyer to the exquisite
drawing-room on the other side, the morning-room
where they had had afternoon tea, and a series of other
rooms, including one that had large chairs and a sofa
between tall bookcases crammed with an eclectic array
of books. It was towards this one that she was headed.

Unfortunately as she stepped on to the wide staircase
she heard voices, realising to her horror that they were
those of Helen and her grandson. They were, she
guessed, standing in the foyer near the drawing-room.

She froze, gingerly backing up the stairs, at the same
time trying to close her ears to the voices that drifted
upwards.

'...don't want anyone to be hurt,' Helen Forsythe was
saying, her autocratic tones overlaid with weariness.

'Gran, no one is going to be hurt.' It should have
sounded soothing, but there was a flat implacable note
in his voice that made Laurel flinch. 'I promise you that.'

'I saw the way she looked at you.'

Laurel could have cringed with shame. She knew
whom they were talking about. Her fingers clenched on
to the banister to stop herself from tripping; she felt as
though her feelings, her wanton stupidity, were being
laid out in the open air for everyone to mock and jeer
at.

Alick laughed cynically. 'Nowadays both sexes are allowed to look, darling. It means nothing. And, even if
it did, don't you think that I can deal with a woman on
the make?'

His grandmother sounded querulous, suddenly old.
'Yes, of course. Only, Alick...'

Suddenly realising what she was doing, Laurel turned
and fled noiselessly back to her room, her scarlet cheeks
and shamed eyes testament to her helpless humiliation.

The fatuous, conceited, egotistical, pompous *beast*,
she thought ferociously, trying to convince herself that
she had never felt forbidden desire for the man who had

dismissed her so contemptuously. How dare he make me sound as though I spent the evening *leering* at him?

But, heartsore and embarrassed though she was, her sense of humour came to her rescue. Her mouth twitched; she leaned into the mirror and contorted her face into a leer of truly villainous dimensions, then gave a sigh of something like resignation and crawled into the iron bed, firmly determined that from now on she was going to treat Alick Forsythe with a cool, composed self-possession that would put him very firmly in his place.

As resolutions went it was a good one, and during the first half of the following day she had no difficulty in keeping it, for the morning was a kaleidoscope of colour and emotion, with telegrams from various political leaders delivered in the mail, friends and family arriving, and the resultant plethora of joyful feelings. Laurel watched with interest and pleasure as her great-aunt and uncle held court, happy, serene, gracious, with their family around them.

Several times her eyes blurred, for it seemed as though it were her own grandmother who sat there, but most of the time she was able to control her emotions enough to enjoy herself.

She met cousins galore, all of whom were curious but affable, and several old-timers from the district who remembered her own grandparents, which was interesting. It was even amusing that without fail all of them spoke of the two runaways with the utmost circumspection, never referring to the scandal that had banished them from this place. It gave her a not unpleasant feeling of timelessness, of the past and the present joining in a way she had never experienced before.

And you a historian! she thought, scoffing. Lifting a glass of champagne to her mouth, she relished the delicious taste, the tiny strings of bubbles that rose through the pale gold liquid. The day was fabulous, one of those magnificent gold and green and blue spring days with a faint fresh wind carrying with it the intense, erotic scent of the citrus flowers.

'I'll never smell orange blossoms again without remembering this occasion,' she said to one of her new-found cousins, a personable young man called Blair Weatherall who was a solicitor in Auckland.

'Mmm, although I think it will always remind me of you,' he said, smiling at her with a lazy intimacy that she acknowledged with a faint smile. 'You're coming to the party tonight, aren't you?'

'The party?'

'Oh, Alick is giving a party for the young, and any of the old who can make it to his place.'

She had forgotten completely the 'party for the young' mentioned in Sophie's letter to her mother. Uncertainly, she said, 'He hasn't said anything——'

'An oversight. Hey, Alick, Laurel thinks she might not be invited to your party tonight. Tell her she is.'

Alick, who had been walking by, turned his steel-sheen gaze on them and replied casually. 'Yes, of course. Sorry, Laurel, I should have made sure you knew all about it.'

'Not to worry,' Blair returned cheerfully. 'I'll pick you up at about six, shall I?'

Alick looked cynically amused as he went on his way, and impelled by a quick flare of anger Laurel said, a little too curtly, 'No, I'll make my own way across, thank you.'

Blair was clearly not accustomed to being turned down. His bright hazel eyes sharpened. 'Nonsense. Be ready at six.'

But Laurel had fought this battle before. Smiling warmly up at him, she said, 'You didn't hear what I said. I'll get myself there, and back again. Understand?'

Blair flushed, but retorted snidely, 'Loud and clear. When did you burn your bra?'

Laurel grinned. 'At the same time you decided that women need to know who's boss.'

The laughter in her expression made him flush even more, but her warmly twinkling eyes worked their usual magic. 'OK,' he sighed, accepting defeat. 'You'd think I'd learn, wouldn't you? My girlfriend slaps me down a lot, too.'

Well parried, she thought, silently applauding his quick retrieval of face.

'However,' he added, watching her with highly suspect casualness, 'if you are thinking of Alick, he's engaged.'

'I know.' She spoke just as offhandedly. 'Jenna and I had a chat last night. A nice woman.'

'Woman? She's still only a kid. But yes, she's a sweet little soul, although we were astounded when he got engaged to her. She's about as unlike his other loves as anyone could be. He used to go for real sophisticates; never had any trouble getting any woman he wanted. Even——' He stopped, his expression rueful, as though he had said more than he intended. A little too quickly, he resumed, 'What is it about the man that makes women drool whenever they see him?'

'Money?' she suggested flippantly.

He rolled his eyes. 'Yeah, I've thought that too, but I know and so do you that it's not the money. The man's got something. Authority, I suppose. What did they use to call it? It! He's got "it". He can be a hard bastard, an ugly customer, but if I ever got into trouble I'd go to him for help.'

'That's—quite a tribute,' she said softly.

His grin was a little self-conscious. 'Oh, well, I like the man. I suffered for years, growing up in his shadow; all we boys did, and all the girls loved him hopelessly, but they had to give up when he started taking out those fantastic creatures. I mean, international models, high-powered businesswomen who frightened the hell out of the rest of us, rich society butterflies from all around the Pacific—you name them, they came running! Then he got himself engaged to Jenna, who's as sweet and wholesome as a bun.'

And about as interesting, his tone implied.

Laurel said lightly, 'Perhaps it's true that a man looks for different attributes when he decides to settle down.'

He sent another sharp look that reminded her he was trained to sum up people. 'I notice you didn't say "fall in love",' he said drily.

She lifted her shoulders in the faintest of shrugs. 'It's the usual reason for marrying, surely,' she parried.

Love, and its bastard brother, lust. For those stupid people who confused the two, misery and pain and anguish fouled the marriage bed.

'Well, I'm damned if I think he's in love with her. He treats her as though she's a sweet little sister——'

Laurel interrupted, 'I don't really think we should be gossiping about them, do you?'

'Clearly,' he pronounced with an expansive gesture that made her wonder just how much champagne he had drunk, 'you don't know the first thing about families. Why, gossip is the sole topic of conversation at these gatherings. Gossip, seasoned with a hefty dose of malice and spite.'

'Nonsense, they're all enjoying themselves far too much for malice and spite.'

He laughed, but said cynically, 'It's there, but they're all on their best behaviour because Alick wouldn't like it if they spoiled his grandparents' party. Still, it's too happy a day to dwell on the darker side of life in a big family. Let's go and get another glass of champagne; then we can sit in the shade of the jacaranda tree, and you can ask me questions about your new-found relatives, and I'll tell you all. With only the merest salting of spite and malice!'

A pleasant weariness claimed Laurel as she went up the stairs in the late afternoon, but it was spiced with an anticipation she was doing her best to repress, because she knew well that it was based on seeing Alick again.

'Stupid, stupid, stupid,' she muttered, as she reached the sanctuary of her room and sat down on the white wicker chair. Stupid, and worse than stupid, because what she was feeling had nothing to do with tender emotions.

This was exactly the way she had reacted to Martin: the avid desire to be with him, the overwhelming of reason by a voracious need, the sweet deceit of desire. And look where that had got her!

Jumping to her feet, she went across to the wardrobe, her small face held in lines of rigid control.

The poverty-stricken years at university had run down her wardrobe, in spite of the dresses her mother had managed to give her at Christmas and birthdays, so she hadn't much in the way of party clothes. With her mouth twisted slightly, she pulled out the silk dress she had worn to dinner the night before and decided that it would have to do for the party. After all, the last thing she wanted to do was look as though she had dressed to attract!

But she washed her hair again, and blow-dried it so that it fell in a shining amber-brown aureole to the nape of her neck. And she made up carefully, using a faint wash of foundation to blend in the freckles, emphasising the slant of her eyes with liner and a mixture of muted green and soft brown shadow, so that they glowed, deep and mysterious, above her high cheekbones.

'Subtle,' she said to herself as she carefully blended and faded the colours together. 'Drama, my dear, is not for you. You're too small.'

A touch of peach to her mouth, and a fleeting wish that it were not quite so wide, and she stepped back, looking at herself with cool, unsparing eyes. A vision of Jenna's face was instantly banished; she knew that she could not compete with such candid prettiness. She had given up futilely longing for what she couldn't have, content to be attractive rather than beautiful. And anyway, she told herself ruthlessly, you don't want to compete with Jenna.

Spraying perfume on to her throat and wrists, she inhaled the exquisite scent of Fidji, her eyes on her reflection. After a moment she shrugged. She looked, she decided with a certain grim satisfaction, every day her age, more than competent to set university examinations and mark them.

The final touch was the dainty Edwardian pendant her grandmother had left her in her will, tiny seed-pearls forming the dangling crescent of a new moon, gold citrines winking around it like tiny stars. All of her life she had loved the charming little conceit; one of her first memories had been as she sat in her grandmother's lap, mesmerised by the smooth sheen of the pearls and the glittering lights in the stones. To go with it she wore pearl studs, a present from her parents on her twenty-first birthday.

Her mouth set into a suspect firmness, she picked up her bag and went down the stairs.

'How nice you look,' Sophie said warmly, appearing from the small sitting-room they called the parlour. 'Fresh and pretty and delicate. Are you coming to say goodbye to the others?'

'Yes, of course.'

They were obviously enjoying a comfortable chat about the day's events, but they welcomed her into their charmed little circle with pleasure. They were, she thought with a sudden rush of affection, awfully nice people, these new relatives of hers. She stayed longer than she should have, not even admitting to herself that she was putting off the moment when she had to leave for the party, but as the cool air of evening seeped in through the open window she heard Aunt Faith say, 'Ah, Laurel, here's Alick, come to pick you up.'

Startled, she looked up and saw him silhouetted against the darkening sky outside. Sternly repressing the sudden leap in her pulses, she got to her feet, pinning on a smile that no one could have called alluring.

'Hello,' she said with brisk impersonal cheerfulness.

Brows lifted, he gave her a mocking smile that faded almost immediately. The arrogant angles of his face tightened; for a moment he stared at her as though she were a stranger, and then his grandmother said something to him and he turned, and the moment was past, lost in the affection that was obvious in his expression as he answered the older woman.

Laurel shivered. She wanted nothing more than to flee back to her bedroom and hide, then return to Auckland and never see, never think of Alick Forsythe again. Panic reeled through her mind, its fumes drugging her, preventing thought, preventing anything but the blind impulse to run.

Stoically, she fought it back, using the next few minutes while his family fondly chatted to him to recover her composure, pulling on the mask of control she had manufactured for herself with such effort.

Then he said, 'Come on, Laurel, otherwise we'll have people banging on the door and wondering if they've come to the right place.'

They left to a chorus of good wishes, but once outside she stopped, puzzled, for there was no car waiting for them.

'I thought we'd walk.' He answered her unspoken query. 'Unless you think it's too far?'

'Oh, no. No, I like walking.'

'And your heels are not too high.'

Was it her imagination, or did his eyes linger on the exposed length of her legs? Keep it light, she adjured herself. Her voice was even as she responded, 'If I wear heels that are at all high they look longer than my legs. And I wobble.'

He chuckled, a warm, oddly intimate sound. 'Really? You look exceptionally well-balanced to me.'

'No, I have this ankle that turns without any warning. Oddly enough, it usually happens when I'm walking on a dead flat surface. It's a nuisance.'

'Perhaps you should exercise it,' he suggested, an undertone of amusement warming his voice.

'I do,' she said briskly. 'Well, some of the time. I tend to forget it for long periods, only starting up exercises once more when I've had another narrow escape from spraining it.'

Why were they talking absurdities? Because it passed the time and kept her from thinking any subversive thoughts, that was why. She went on chattily, 'It's been a lovely day, hasn't it? Everything went well.'

'Yes. No one got drunk, no one mortally offended anyone; even those who hate each other behaved with propriety. And the weather co-operated magnificently. As you say, it's been a success.'

Somewhat startled, she said, 'That's exactly the sort of thing Blair said. Aren't you both being a little cynical? I suppose there are a few who dislike each other, but hatred? Isn't that a little strong?'

'Not in the least. I'm sorry if I shatter any rosy illusions, but families are not all sweetness and light, and yours is not the only feud in the family.'

'Well, yes, but...' She gestured vaguely. 'I suppose it's just that I'm not accustomed to big families. Everyone seemed to be having such fun.'

'Naturally.' The word was delivered with a cool deliberation that made her shrivel. 'Apart from anything else, they know damned well that I wouldn't allow anyone to spoil a very important occasion for my grandparents. Incidentally, Blair is almost engaged to a woman who is at the moment on holiday in Rarotonga.'

'Yes, I know,' she said absently, then did a double-take. 'Why?' she asked with a crisp hauteur that brought her head up abruptly.

'Just a friendly warning. He might be attracted to the idea of a flirtation, but that's all it would be. He's been besotted with Petra for the last two years.'

She shrugged, hating him for the unkind derision in his tone. 'Don't worry, he's a nice chap, but I'm not in the habit of conducting flirtations with men I hardly know, or those who are committed to someone else.'

'No?' he asked gently.

Memories of several heated exchanges of glances fuelled her belligerent reply. 'No.' There, that would tell him, as openly as she dared, that she had no intention of following up on that forbidden wildfire attraction. 'Besides,' she added, just to hammer it home, 'I don't suppose I'll be seeing any of the family again after this until the next diamond wedding anniversary.'

'Oh, I doubt that very much.' His voice was dry. 'Now that you have made the contact it would be foolish of you to back off, surely.'

'I don't know what you mean,' she said blankly.

'I know you have no other relatives, because your father was an orphan.'

'How do you know that?' she counter-attacked fiercely. But her agile mind had already supplied the answer. Rage and incredulity jerked her to a stop. Turning to face him, she clenched her hands into small fists by her sides. 'You had us investigated,' she spat.

He, too, had stopped, dark brows raised as he surveyed her face through the rapidly darkening air. 'Of course,' he said, sounding faintly surprised, 'As soon as Gran began to talk about you. I love my grandparents— I was not going to have them upset if you and your mother turned out to be a pair of undesirables. Which could have happened; even the best families have them.'

Her breath scalded in her lungs. Temper, hot and uncontrollable, raced through her; she had to tighten her small fists so that she wouldn't make the hideous mistake of striking the small taunting smile from his cruel mouth.

It took her several tense moments before she could regain sang-froid enough to say scathingly, 'I suppose I should be grateful that we got an invitation. After all, we may not be exactly *undesirable*,' her voice underlined the word with scorn and contempt, 'but we certainly aren't in the same echelon as the rest of your precious relatives.'

His hand snaked out and caught her chin, holding it in fingers that bit deeply as he said with harsh distinctness, 'We are not snobs, *cousin*. I don't give a damn how much money you have—or haven't—but I must admit that I didn't like the sound of your first marriage.'

She went white to the lips. In the dark his eyes were cold and hard, stabbing into her mind with a force that couldn't be denied. Trying to quell a deep, inchoate fear, she drew a trembling breath and demanded, 'Why?'

He shrugged, distaste colouring his tones. 'I never liked Martin Du Fresne.'

'You knew him,' she whispered, dazed, her defiance foundered in a sea of pain.

His face was a stark etching, cold and closed against her. 'I know him. I went to school with his cousin.'

'Oh, God, the old school tie,' she said bitterly. 'No wonder you had us investigated. I'll bet your private detective got an earful from Martin's mother. She was particularly scathing about my lack of breeding.' Her mouth stretched in a meaningless smile. 'Ironic, isn't it, that I could have claimed you as a cousin? I'm sure that that would have smoothed my path considerably.'

'Breeding means nothing,' he said with a crack like a whip in the harsh voice, 'unless it's allied to character. You married Martin Du Fresne for his money——'

She flung her head back and laughed, the sound of it shocking in the quiet evening. 'Is that what she told you? I always thought she had ice-water in her veins. Well, she couldn't have been more wrong! I married Martin because I wanted to go to bed with him, and because I'd been brought up to believe that nice girls didn't sleep with men unless they were prepared to marry them.'

'So what went wrong? Why did he leave you?'

Another lie from Martin's mother. Laurel had been the one who had left. She stared at him, her mouth set in a straight hard line, angry because she had already said more than she had intended. 'I don't have to tell you anything about my marriage, except that it was the biggest mistake I've ever made.'

She cried out as his hand contracted on the tender bones of her chin. With a muttered oath he released her, almost flinging her away as though she contaminated him.

'Precious little compassion or sympathy in you, is there?' he snarled. 'The man's dead, killed parachuting off a mountain, and all you can say is that he was a mistake.'

Wincing, she continued to hold her head high. Not for anything would she tell him one sordid detail of that year of marriage.

Martin hadn't wanted her to have any sort of life that didn't have him enshrined as its focal point and god. And the only proof of her love he had been prepared to accept was her response in bed. But that was what she hadn't been able to give him.

All the desire, the urgent need that had pushed her pell-mell into marriage, had vanished. She was hopeless in bed. Her confidence driven away, her self-esteem undermined, she had endured her husband's cruelty, his rough passion, until finally she had been unable to bear it and had fled back home.

A cold shiver caught her unawares. 'You know nothing,' she said thinly, and turned away.

'Where are you going?' He sounded oddly shaken, the rough words coming too quickly.

'Back to the house.'

'No. I don't want you worrying my grandparents by returning so soon.'

'I won't worry them. I'll just say that—that I have a headache,' she finished curtly.

'I'm sure you'll have no difficulty in lying to them, but no.' And when she made to move he caught her upper arm, holding her still.

Freezing, she waited like a small animal, wary and tense, aware that she hadn't the strength to free herself, and alert for the moment when his concentration lapsed and she could break away.

'They're not stupid,' he said grimly, holding her eyes with his. 'If you go back to the house they're going to know that we've argued, and I don't want that. For some reason, it's important for Gran that she keeps in contact with your mother and you. So, you'll come with me now, and when you've stayed an hour or so you can go back and plead a headache.'

She measured his expression, tilted eyes hooded beneath the thick fringe of her lashes, her brain working furiously. That first instinct, to tell him to go to hell and take his autocratic temperament with him, died. He looked more than tough and arrogant; standing over her he looked lethal, the flat planes and harsh angles of his face set into an expression of implacable determination, the steel-blue gaze ruthlessly imperative.

Slowly, her eyes fixed on to his face, she said, 'All right. Now let me go.'

She was going to have marks on her skin tomorrow, but he looked with surprise at his lean fingers biting into her arm as though he hadn't even known he was grasping her so mercilessly.

'I—all right,' he said distantly, releasing her as though she burned his fingers. 'I'm sorry.'

'It's all right.' Still fuming, but shaken, her heart scurrying in her chest, she resumed her way towards his house, not bothering to see whether he came with her or not.

Although he made no sound on the short grass, she knew when he had caught her up. She could feel him walking beside her with that dangerous litheness, sense the intensely male aura that sizzled around him, and had to keep reminding herself that it was just that same virile authority that had attracted her to Martin.

It had turned out to be the super-confident shield of a weak man; it could be exactly the same here, she thought cattily, knowing, even as the thought formulated in her brain, that she was wrong. There was more to Alick than the arrogant power-seeking of a man who needed to conquer and humiliate in order to feed his own shaky esteem.

The house was still empty, but the first car came up the drive as Alick pushed open the door. Surprisingly, it had Jenna in it, her pretty face hardening when she saw Laurel there.

'Oh, you should have told me to pick Laurel up,' she said, smiling with a little less friendliness than before as she came up to them. 'I'm sorry, I should have thought of it and then you wouldn't have had to go across, darling.'

She pulled Alick's head down and kissed him seductively. Tactfully, Laurel turned away, aware that he pulled free almost immediately, not abruptly, but with a deliberation that made it obvious he didn't like public embraces.

Probably, like Martin, he was the sort of man who had to take the initiative in lovemaking, Laurel thought snidely, repressing the outraged jealousy that ripped through her at the thought of Jenna's soft mouth clinging to his. And more than probably he had noticed the sideways triumphant look that Jenna had sent her way just before she kissed him. Macho men like Alick—and Martin—didn't like proprietorial women.

The party should have been fun. Everyone was certainly there to enjoy themselves, and they all knew each other. Laurel managed to convince herself that she too was having a good time. By staying well away from Alick and Jenna she could give all her attention to the people she was talking to; pleasant people, as curious as she was about the long sundering of the two family lines, who were prepared to welcome their cousin into their casually amiable friendships. And, in spite of Alick's and Blair's comments, she didn't see any signs of hatred or dislike.

After a while, and especially as Alick didn't come near her, she gave up the idea of going back to the homestead. Her mother would ask numerous questions about the family and she wanted to be able to answer them correctly, so she settled down to take mental notes.

Blair stayed fairly close to her. At first she accepted his company cautiously, but when it became clear that he had given up any idea of a flirtation she relaxed, enjoying his drily caustic comments on the assembled partygoers and the snippets of information he fed her, most of them sharply perceptive but qualified with affection.

It was he who said, 'Wonder what's got into Jenna tonight? If she weren't such a virtuous soul I'd say she's been hitting the champagne. She doesn't normally hang on to Alick like that, all over him like a rash. He's such a poker-face you'd never know from looking at him, but I'll bet he's not enjoying it much.'

'They are engaged,' she said with a note of acid. 'A little closeness is obligatory, surely.'

He grinned. 'Alick is not like we lesser mortals,' he intoned. 'Even with Michelle—well, especially with Michelle, I suppose, seeing as she was married—oops! Oh, God, I've had too much to drink!' Mortified, he set down the glass of wine in his hand.

Laurel gave him an astonished look then said quickly, 'Don't tell me, I don't want to know.'

'I'll have to,' he said miserably, 'because, thanks to my big mouth and too much alcohol, I've managed to give you the wrong impression totally. Michelle was married, but her husband had left her before she and Alick had the affair.'

'In that case, one wonders why her husband left her.'

Blair said truculently, 'I've never believed the gossip. Alick does not break up marriages. He's as straight as a die, with a moral code that could give the Puritans some points. Hard, perhaps a little too proud, and he leaves married women strictly alone.'

But there was a note in his voice that made Laurel look closely at him. She realised, with a dismay that was surely quite unnecessary, that Blair did not believe a word of what he was saying. So, Alick and this Michelle had had a flaming affair and Blair was convinced that it had broken up Michelle's marriage. And this was the man who told her he didn't like the sound of her marriage, who had had her investigated!

She should feel disgust, scorn, even contempt; but all she could recognise was a strange cold anger.

She hid it by shrugging, saying lightly, 'Never mind, Blair, I know you didn't mean to tell me, so I won't remember it. Now, tell me who that raving beauty over there is, the young siren with the sulky, sultry face and the hair like burgundy flame.'

'That is the family black sheep. Her name is Aura Forsythe and she belongs to a cousin of grandfather's.'

'She looks a bit young to be a black sheep. How old is she, sixteen?'

He was obviously glad to follow this lead away from the dangerous topic of Alick's affair. 'Yes, about that. Certainly no older. My dear, she was the family black sheep by the time she reached twelve! Mind you, she had a fairly tough time of it. Her father divorced her mother and took off for service in Africa when Aura was about eight. I don't think he's ever been back. Her mother remarried a couple of years later, and the new stepfather and Aura didn't get on, so they sent her away to boarding-school, and she ran away so often they gave up in the end and let her live with her grandmother. But the iron had entered into her soul by then. Fortunately Alick has no difficulty controlling her, although she doesn't regard him with the same awe as the rest of us, believe me.'

No, Laurel thought, surveying the stubborn chin and the vivid intelligent gaze, this one would not be in awe of many.

CHAPTER THREE

SOMEONE put a tape on and, before Laurel knew it, she was dancing with Blair. The music kept playing and she kept dancing, going from cousin to cousin, smiling, laughing, parrying flirtatious remarks with swift wit, letting the music and the movement blot out everything else.

Until, inevitably, she and Alick were dancing together, and the mindless enjoyment became transmuted into something darker, menacing at the same time that it thrilled, a sudden submerged vein of desire beating in time with the music, subversive, almost terrifying.

One hand was firm on her back, the other aloofly enclosing hers. Their steps matched; she had to fight to keep her eyes open, the weighted lids apart, as she tensed to the brush of his thighs against her, the heat of his body and the scent of him, faint, elusive, yet so masculinely arousing that it tormented her nerve-ends into open response.

This, she acknowledged painfully, was something new. She had thought she wanted Martin but his presence had not swamped her in sensation so piercing that it was almost anguish. Her lashes lifted; she darted Alick a fleeting glance. He was not looking at her. Instead, his gaze was directed above her head, his face as impassive as a sculpture carved in granite.

Only someone very close by would notice the tiny muscle flicking in his jaw.

Laurel's lashes fell. Sheer panic made her witless. For a few moments she could only think, What will I do? Oh, what will I do?

Then her tough common sense reasserted itself. All right, so she was painfully vulnerable to him, but she

57

was in control of her life now, she was no stupid little twenty-year-old at the mercy of her hormones.

Admit it, she told herself; go on, admit that you want him. You want Alick Forsythe. Go on, say, I want Alick Forsythe. It wasn't hard, was it? Now, say something else: He is engaged to Jenna.

She murmured a breathless apology after missing a step, and tried once more to ignore the flexion of the muscles in his thigh as he caught her against him and whirled her expertly around. Prickles of sensation stabbed through her skin, deep into her body, gathering in a delicious irritation in the pit of her stomach. It burgeoned into an ache, hot and sweet and tumultuous. Savagely she bit into her bottom lip, willing the pain to banish the hunger, wild and fierce, that held her in thrall.

It didn't work, so she closed her eyes. But instantly there flashed on the darkness a *mélange* of images so boldly erotic that she gasped, and her lashes flew up again above rapidly colouring cheeks.

'Sorry,' he said, the deep voice infuriatingly impersonal.

Stop it, she commanded her over-active imagination, and in a voice as smooth as cream she asked. 'What for?'

'You winced, so I assumed I'd trodden on your toe.'

'No. You're an excellent dancer.'

'So are you.'

Polite trivialities, but at least they took her mind off dangerous territory.

'Tell me,' he murmured, 'what you think of the present political situation.'

The sheer irrelevance of the command, for command it had definitely been, widened her eyes. She met the unsettling gleam in his with confusion. Then she realised that he had offered a way out. Perhaps the tension was getting to him too, or possibly he was just trying to tip her off balance. Whatever the reason, she seized on his words with relief and told him exactly what she thought of the present political situation, making her comments as provocative as possible.

He listened with a sardonic little smile curling that hard mouth, and answered in kind. Accustomed to defending her point of view, Laurel relished the cut and thrust of discussion, and arguing with Alick was exhilarating. He had a mind like a razor and he picked up her every small error in logic, forcing her to justify views she had held for years.

But it was not all one-sided. Even as the music played seductively on, she found herself verbally pinning him down, doing exactly the same to him. Her eyes sparkled with anticipation; she almost forgot the potent carnal spell woven about her in the pleasure of debating with a man whose outlook was not, she discovered, so fundamentally different from hers; for all that, he taunted her with being a sickly liberal while she loftily scorned his views as conservative and reactionary.

She could almost forget the slow counterpoint beneath the quick interplay of minds; the smooth co-ordination of bodies, the hidden subliminal response that began at a cellular level, yet, in some mysterious way, transcended the merely physical.

When at last the music ended it was to laughter from him and a sparkling upward glance from her, unconscious mischief radiating from the glowing topaz depths of her eyes.

His face hardened; he said formally, 'Thank you,' and took her across to where Blair was sitting and flirting with the bewitching Aura.

'Oh, Alick!' she cried, jumping up in a flurry of skirts about long tanned legs. 'Alick, I have to talk to you! Mum is being——'

'Manners,' he admonished, smiling at her with an easy affection that seemed to belie Blair's reading of their relationship.

The full, sulky mouth tightened, but Aura turned politely back to Laurel. 'Sorry,' she sighed. 'Alick is the

only person who'll listen to me without clucking his
tongue and saying, "Oh, *Aura!*"'

Laurel liked him for that, although a nasty part of
her mind decided that no man would find a tête-à-tête
with such a lovely girl a hardship.

She grinned. 'Go ahead and unburden yourself,' she
said cheerfully. 'Good big brothers are hard to come by,
so it pays to snatch the opportunity to sob on the
shoulder of one whenever you can.'

Aura looked at her more closely, a spark of surprised
speculation glimmering in the great green eyes. 'Thanks,'
she said simply, and smiled.

She was breathtakingly beautiful. Laurel firmly
squashed the pang of ignoble envy that such loveliness
aroused, her eyes faintly sombre as she watched the
couple move off, Aura talking rapidly and earnestly, her
slender hand unconsciously massaging the whipcord
strength of Alick's forearm.

'In five years' time,' Blair said cheerfully, 'when she
really starts to learn what she can do with a face and
body like that, God help the men she wants.'

Laurel returned calmly, 'And heaven help her if she
hasn't gained some sophistication by then, because she'll
be earning it the hard way.'

'Spoken with feeling,' he observed, his eyes still on
his cousin. 'Did it come hard to you, Laurel?'

'Doesn't it to everyone?' she parried, giving nothing
away.

'Perhaps. Oh-oh. Here's trouble.'

Her attention caught by the knowing, amused note in
his voice, she followed his gaze. Jenna had come up to
Alick and Aura and waylaid them; she was smiling, but
even from across the room her tension was obvious.

'Green-eyed jealous,' Blair said in an undertone.
'Jenna's actually quite possessive in a quiet way, but I
suppose if you spend a fair amount of time wondering
why the man you love chose you out of all the women
in the world, you're bound to be insecure. Pity she can't

hide it. Aura's not such a close cousin—about the same relationship as you, actually—but anyone can see that Alick is only purely and paternally interested in her. He's not into cradle-snatching. Wonder how he's going to get out of this.'

Very smoothly. He said something that made both women laugh, then Jenna went across the room with them before detaching herself with an understanding look at Alick from beneath her lashes and a remark that set Aura bristling balefully but only brought a faint smile to his impassive face.

It was probably her imagination that read anger into his expression, Laurel decided, because he certainly revealed no outward sign of it. And the smile he gave his young cousin was lazy and faintly teasing.

Yet she was sure that he was furious. Body language? How could it be? He was too far away for her to discern the tiny muscle movements that registered so subtly with the onlooker's subconscious.

'Well done, Alick. A few words, smiles all round, and not a drop of blood on the floor.' Blair's voice was a welcome intrusion into her thoughts. He laughed and continued, 'You can stop staring. Have to hand it to Alick, he can defuse an obstreperous little cousin and a possessive fiancée just as easily as he makes a killing on the stock market. Whatever he's got, I wish it ran in the family!'

Recalled to herself, Laurel made some flippant response, and dragged her eyes away from the couple by now ensconced just outside the wide glass doors that led out on to the sitting-out area and the pool with its waterfall. Aura was still talking, her incredible eyes fixed on to her cousin's face with what appeared to be painful intensity.

Something ugly stirred in Laurel's breast, and was overcome. Jealousy was a despicable, nasty emotion, one she was not going to give in to.

Martin had been jealous, in an odd way. He had sneered at her friends and family, telling her that as his wife it was her duty to mix with his friends, none of whom she had liked. They had all seemed frivolous and shallow—some, she had sensed, even vicious—but in the end it had seemed easier to give up protesting and accept the stringent limitations he had clamped around her life.

She hadn't, though. Some small, courageous part of her had seen what was happening and had fought it.

It had been ugly. Fear had made her brutal; she had left him flatly, refusing to attend marriage guidance, refusing to see him, even though her mother had pleaded with her. She had been cruel because she had been terrified of what he was doing to her. And she had never regretted leaving; her greatest regrets were saved for the fact that she had been stupid enough to marry him when she hadn't really known him.

Even when she realised that he was telling everyone that *he* had left *her*, she had refused to counter his claims with the truth. Let him save what he could of his pride. She had no need of it.

An ironic little smile twisted her mouth into a grimace. But he did. It was only his pride that had been hurt because she couldn't respond to him. So he had called her unfeminine, a tease, a frigid little whore, because that was what whores did: they promised the earth and remained aloof from the whole business.

It still hurt, especially as it had begun to seem that he might have been right. In spite of the need that still racked her body, the thought of actually enduring the intimacies of making love made her shudder.

'Cold?' Blair got to his feet and extended a hand. 'Come and dance some more; that'll warm you up.'

The coldness was not physical; it came from deep inside, but she couldn't tell him that. With a smile, she allowed herself to be escorted into the middle of the room and swept into the crowd which was dancing there.

Much later, she decided that she was ready to go back to the homestead. Her head ached, and from the faint buzzing in her ears she deduced that she'd had a little too much champagne to drink. The party was still humming along, everyone obviously enjoying themselves very much. Averting her eyes from the sight of Alick and Jenna locked together in an embrace that was only sanctioned by the music, she slid away from the noisy group she had been talking to for half an hour or so and make her way across to Blair.

'I think I'll head back now,' she said lightly. 'Can you tell Alick I've gone? I'll see him tomorrow, no doubt, and I'll thank him then.'

'I'll take you back,' he said instantly, not bothering to hide the glint in his eye.

Her small face was sunnily amused as she wrinkled her nose at him. 'Now, what harm could come to me walking through the orange groves? You stay; I want a little peace and quiet while I make my way back.'

He grinned, but made no further offers. After bidding him goodnight, she made her way across the room and slid through the door without being noticed by anyone.

Outside it was cool and still, a moon as thin and pearly as the one on her pendant sinking rapidly into the west. Carried on a whisper of breeze, the scent of the orange blossoms hung heavily on the air, sweet and disturbing, setting her nerve-ends quivering uneasily.

But then, she was already nervous; had been ever since her eyes first met Alick's intimidating gaze. Astonishing that it had only been yesterday! And this time tomorrow, she reminded herself with hard, practical common sense, she was going to be back where she belonged and she wouldn't see or meet Alick Forsythe again. So she would soon forget the fact that she wanted him with every cell in her body.

Still strung up, she reached the dark silent house and went upstairs, walking softly and swiftly into her quiet room. Without putting on the light she stripped, slowly

removing her clothes and shoes before pulling on a thin
wrap as she went across to the window. For several
minutes she stood looking out at the pools of darkness
and light that were the garden below, and along the
darkened rows of orange trees. Music drifted through
the orchard, rendered soft and almost plaintive by distance, the thin strands of melody backed by a deep,
throbbing beat.

She wouldn't get to sleep yet. It was only too easy to
see Jenna and Alick dancing, her arms wound around
his neck, her eyes lifted worshipfully to his, his mouth
relaxed into an odd little smile as they moved perfectly
together. Two splendid golden people, much better suited
than she and Martin had been.

Martin had enjoyed her smallness; it had satisfied
some sort of need in him. Perhaps the need to dominate.

Muttering an oath, Laurel turned away and slipped
across the hall to the bathroom, hoping to find, in the
soothing, familiar routine of preparing for bed, some
surcease from the wild tides surging through her body,
and the bitter memories.

But even when she had put away her clothes and was
clad in the thin cotton T-shirt she wore to bed, she was
still a prisoner of the restlessness that thrummed through
her. Frowning, she switched on her bedside lamp, taking
up a book she had had the forethought to remove from
the library that afternoon. By dint of some superhuman
concentration she managed to lose herself in it.

It could have been an hour later that she yawned, and
set it down again. By then the unnaturally sharp, febrile
excitation of the party seemed to have died down to a
pleasant lethargy, the sound of the distant music having
faded, so, presumably, it was over. She looked at her
watch—two-thirty in the morning. Not wildly late, but
not early, either. Restraining herself from wandering
back to the window, she yawned and doused the lamp
with a sharp click.

She was curled up in bed before she realised that she hadn't taken out the pearl studs in her ears. Her brows drawn together, she removed the earrings and, switching on the lamp, got up to put them into their box. Beside it another box gaped at her, the dark worn velvet reproachful in its emptiness. Her heart dropped. Her hand stole to touch the skin of her throat, stroking tentatively across the smooth warmth to meet only emptiness. Her grandmother's pendant was gone.

The thin gold chain must have broken some time during the night. Perhaps when she had been walking back across the orchard, because she surely would have noticed if it had fallen at Alick's house. Surely? How could she have not noticed?

Only too easily, she told herself contemptuously; you were too busy getting into a sexual frenzy over your cousin!

She hesitated, wondering what to do. Her first impulse was to race outside and quarter the ground across the orchard, but of course that would be stupid at this late hour. There was too little light to see the fragile thing in the dark, and she had no idea where to find a torch. Blinking back a rush of hot tears, she disciplined her emotions. It would have to wait until morning; much as she valued the only thing her grandmother had left her, she was not going back to the house where Alick lived with Jenna.

A soft noise outside her door made her freeze. After a second her heart steadied enough for her to realise that it probably came from outside and she relaxed. Then again, lightly, almost noiselessly, someone tapped on her door.

Her breath locked in her throat. For a moment she stared unbelievingly at the unresponsive wood, then with a harsh shake of her head managed to force herself across to the door. She opened it a fraction, to meet the shock of Alick's gaze with a queer sense of inevitability. He was leaning against the wall, loose, relaxed; yet she sensed the tension and the power beneath the pose of supple grace, and her heartbeat sped up. From the fingers of one lean hand dangled the pendant, seed-pearls shimmering in the subdued hall light.

He straightened, his eyes dwelling with savage intentness on the heart-shaped contours of her face. A *frisson* of sensation ran through her. Nervously she moistened her mouth, then said, with an effort that produced a disturbing huskiness, 'Thank you. I'd just missed it.'

'Did you know, my grandmother has one exactly the same, except that the stones are peridots?'

'No,' she whispered.

'They got them on their eighteenth birthday.'

She nodded, then held out her hand. He dropped the pendant into her palm, folding her fingers over it. It was like being burned by a current of electricity, sparking from his hand to hers, scorching through her blood, setting fire to her heart.

Dragging in a quick, ragged breath she said, 'Thank you.'

His hand was still around hers, warm, strong, trapping a willing prisoner. The air seemed to throb with unbearable tension between them. Like two wild animals locked in a silent struggle for mastery, they stood motionless, facing each other, eyes clinging, both faces expressionless. As though in a trance she felt his index finger move across and touch the pulse that beat like a tiny kettledrum at her wrist.

'Damn!' he said, with all the intense ferocity of a curse, and then she was in his arms and his mouth was on hers, sweet as the temptations of an unholy paradise, drugging her into mindless acquiescence.

It was like a rapid descent into unconsciousness, but in this dazed, silent world of the senses she was only too aware.

Logic, reason, common sense...all the hard-won attributes of the higher mind fled into chaos. Sighing, her small body taut with anticipation, she pressed herself against him, her pulses dancing in uninhibited excitement. His mouth was hard, even slightly cruel, and more than a little reckless as though, having given in to the urge they had both been repressing for the last two days, he was determined to exact the utmost pleasure from it.

When he lifted his head she made a tiny broken sound of need, and he laughed beneath his breath and whispered, 'Open your mouth to me. Let me in.'

For a moment she froze, but he kissed her ear, his breath whispering into the sensitive whorls with erotic force, and when his mouth reached hers again she obeyed without demur, letting him gain access to the sweet depths, racked with delicious anticipation by the quick thrust of his tongue, responding with a sharp twist of her hips.

His obvious arousal excited her. Her hands clenched in his dark honey hair, then slid down, past the strong column of his neck, spreading as wide as they could across the bunched muscles of his shoulders.

Even as she sighed into his mouth she was gripped by a sense of power; this man, so much bigger than she was, so potent in his masculinity, was trembling against her as she trembled, completely at the mercy of a desire that was increasing exponentially, a savage leftover from the dark primitive days of instinct and emotion. They strained together, breast against chest, hips welded in a surging need for the sated oblivion that only mating would bring.

The world spun when he lifted her, and righted itself as she was laid on the bed. Perhaps she should have used that brief moment to rally her defences, but by the time she had shaken off the sensual languor that flowed, smooth as honey, through her bones he had wrenched off his shirt and was down beside her, kissing the tender line of her throat while his hand pushed up the soft worn cotton of her T-shirt.

The moan died stillborn in her throat. She thought
that she might die if he stopped, and then his mouth
discovered the tender mound of her breast and she knew
she would die if he kept on kissing her. Strange tides
surged in her blood, heated, slow with the weight of ages,
new and fresh as tomorrow. Sensations arrowed through
her to pool in a hot, heavy ache of need between her
thighs. She sighed and turned her head to kiss his
shoulder, running her tongue with delicate greed across
the tight bulge of a muscle.

He tasted of salt, and smelt of aroused male. She
whispered his name and bit at his skin, sucking gently
as he suckled her, his mouth causing an incredible shaft
of sensation to pierce her through and through.

He lifted her, his hands shaking when they wrenched
the T-shirt over her head so that he could feast his eyes
on the rounded womanly curves centred by tightly beaded
aureoles pleading for the renewed attention of his mouth.

Dazzled by the novelty of her response, and even more
by the dark masculinity that clung to him like an aura,
she pulled him down to her, running her hands with eager
greed across his chest, her fingers seeking with wanton
pleasure the hard male contours, the erotic satisfying
strength of his body.

He had turned the light off, so she could barely see
him, but the fire in his eyes scorched her, holding her
pinned like a sacrifice for his gaze.

Muttering something that sounded like an oath, he
sought her mouth with his, driving into it with some of
the force of the embrace his kiss simulated. Laurel held
nothing back, responding with the same fierce need,
totally lost to everything but the imperatives of her body.
His arms were hard as iron across her back as her small
slender form arched fiercely into his, welcoming the solid
weight, the fire of his need and her own.

For a long moment they lay welded together in a
heated, mindless embrace, until he lifted his mouth and
asked softly, 'Is this what you want, Laurel? For me to

take you, here? Get dressed, and we can go back to my house; and then, sweet sensualist, you can let go and scream when I take you.'

For long seconds the words did not sink in, but when at last they did she was overtaken by a wave of nausea so intense that she thought she might be forced to give in to it.

Her lashes fluttered down over her eyes, hiding the shame. She said in a low, humiliated voice, 'I didn't re-alise that you liked to indulge in group sex, Alick. You might be able to persuade Jenna into it, but I draw the line before there.'

Above her hands his chest lifted sharply, then sank. She dropped her hands as though he were red-hot and shrank away. Small as she was she had learned from bitter experience that men were strong and that their anger could become quickly transmuted into action. Not that Martin had ever beaten her, but he had not been gentle, and she had little hope of defending herself in this vulnerable position.

But Alick made no attempt to hurt her, to force himself on to her shrinking flesh. 'Jenna isn't there,' he said silkily.

For a moment an exquisite relief raced through her, but the respite from lovemaking had allowed her to summon up some will-power. 'However she *is* engaged to you,' she said, resistance flattening her tone. 'And this should never have happened.'

He was very still. Then a small, feral smile played about that cruel mouth. One hand curved about her breast, dark against light, calloused strength imprisoning delicate voluptuousness. The other hand locked about her throat. He didn't hurt her—he was quite gentle—yet there was such menace in the slow movements that the breath was stopped in her throat.

'No,' he said softly, bending his head so that the breath played warmly over her navel. 'But we both know it's been brewing ever since we laid eyes on each other, don't we?'

'Alick, don't.' To her humiliation, the words came out in a soft plea.

It was a plea that was ignored. Very slowly, he began to taste the skin around her navel, his lips barely touching the taut silkiness in caresses that were like the brushing of a butterfly's wing. It was torture of the most refined sort, a long drawn-out sensual intimidation that had her nerves screaming.

'Admit it,' he said softly, his breath purring across the violently sensitised skin.

'You know it has,' she said desperately. Racked by an intolerable need her body suddenly stiffened, but he must have read the signs because he lifted his head.

She whispered, 'Please, stop it,' but even as she shuddered his mouth began again, teasing, tormenting, in a mocking, hateful mimicry of love-play.

Gathering up her strength she tried to wrench herself free, but his hand tightened at her throat, just enough to warn her, and she subsided back into a sullen quiescence, beginning to panic now for his deadly intentness was terrifying.

Yet, for all the far from subtle threat, the soft brush of his mouth across her skin set up a thick throbbing throughout her body, an aching hunger that centred in the fork of her body, driving her crazy. Once more she straightened out, swift as an arrow freed from bondage by the bow, desperate to ease the need; and, once more, he avoided it, laughing beneath his breath as she lay panting, her eyes fixed ferociously on him, her heart fluttering madly beneath the heel of his hand.

That was when he added a tiny refinement. His thumb brushed softly across the too-sensitive peak of her breast, awakening such a clamour of desire that she began to shiver, deep tremors rising from the traitor buried in her body... cold, until she was rendered helpless in a wave of heat.

Then, when she thought she would go mad and scream with frustration, his mouth clamped down on to her navel and his tongue thrust in. She shook in a fever of need, tears glittering beneath her lashes, hating him, hating herself for being so humiliatingly defenceless against his sexual harassment. Frustration clawed at her, rending her, throwing her to the wolves of her desire.

'Sleep well,' he said pleasantly, and got up and left the room.

She turned her head to see the stones in the pendant glittering in the starlight through the window, tiny, winking glints of light, as cold as his parody of passion.

He was at church the next day, his angular face austere and expressionless, the hard mouth unsoftened by any memory of the wild emotions of the night before. Jenna stood beside him with a sweet, taut smile. For one searing moment Laurel damned him a hypocrite with her glance, before she turned away and kept her gaze firmly off him, refusing to allow his presence to spoil the service.

Afterwards they ate at the homestead, a relaxed, lazily replete lunch with family only. It was a pity that Laurel couldn't taste any of the superb food for Samma Johnson, the housekeeper, had excelled herself, serving crayfish salad and a wonderful scallop dish, as well as the splendid fresh fruit and vegetables of the north.

By dint of some skilful manoeuvring Laurel kept well away from Alick, but occasionally their eyes met. She hoped that hers gave away as little as his guarded, faintly sardonic blandness, but she feared that her body's instinctive response was only too obvious to the man who had given her more excitement with his controlled, forbidden caresses than any of Martin's impassioned loving.

And she couldn't help seeing that Jenna was still watching her with a suspicion she recognised only too well. Guilt ate at her, combining with a hateful shame to deaden the golden sparkle in her eyes and tighten the soft line of her mouth.

She had vowed never to be persuaded into such a degrading mixture of emotions again, and she hated Alick Forsythe for being able to break so easily through her defences. But she hated him more, she admitted with a small inner shudder, for not feeling the same ungovernable desire. Coolly and dispassionately he had made love to her with a cynical intention to punish, and he had succeeded.

Now he knew that she had had no defences against him, while he was very able to restrain whatever passion he felt. It was inhuman; she felt like a woman who had offered everything and had had it thrown back in her face with casual, deliberate cruelty.

So it was a relief when she left early in the afternoon. Although her new-found relatives urged her to return as soon as she could, she had the feeling that perhaps her great-aunt Helen was not averse to her departure. Those acute eyes had registered that there was something amiss, and that it was connected to her grandson.

Eagerness to be free of them all didn't make her discourteous. Smiling, she said her goodbyes, thanked them all for making such a perfect weekend of it, even managed to keep her voice steady as she shook Alick's lean hand and smiled full into his hard-planed face, the smooth, lying words rolling steadily from her tongue.

'It's been such fun,' she said, ignoring the heated flicker of incandescence in her bloodstream as his fingers closed around hers. She held his heavy-lidded stare for just one limpid moment too long. 'So interesting,' she murmured.

His mouth tightened, then twisted, and before she could wrench her hand free he had lifted it to his mouth and kissed the back of it.

At least it must have *looked* like a kiss. Only she registered the swift, fierce nip of his teeth on her skin.

She jerked it away and managed an admiring upward tilt of her head. 'Done with grace and style,' she said tightly. 'My mother will be thrilled to know that such an old-fashioned gesture hasn't been entirely lost.'

She turned on her heel and slid into the car, set the engine going, and, with one wave, took off down the drive. Damn him, damn him, damn him!

Her body had reacted with a sudden lurch of desire, and he had known it, for she had recognised the cold, hostile satisfaction in his steel-blue eyes.

The trip back was tiring, her frustrated emotions and the sleepless night catching up with her; and then she had to suffer through her mother's gentle but inexorable inquest, telling her about as much of the weekend's events as she could while censoring her own reactions, pretending that she had enjoyed herself immensely. Her bread-and-butter letter to her great-aunt was a little stiff, but she wrote it quickly then set her mind to putting the whole unsettling episode behind her.

She thought she had succeeded but when, some weeks later, she glanced up from the exam paper she was working on, it was to find her mother looking at her with a worried expression.

'Darling,' Mrs Webster said earnestly, 'what is the matter with you? You've been—well, *distracted*—ever since you came back from Kerikeri.'

Laurel smothered a sigh. So much for hiding her emotions! 'I met a man,' she said, adding quickly, before her mother could say anything, 'The wrong man.'

'I see.' The older woman looked even more worried. 'I should be glad—I'd begun to wonder whether you were ever going to meet a man you could like. Why was he wrong?'

'Well, to start off with he looked a bit like Martin. Unfortunately the lean, rangy, arrogant type seems to press all the right buttons with me. Then, he was engaged.'

Mrs Webster made no attempt to hide her sigh. 'What a pity. What was he like?'

Firmly repressing memories of a mouth that conjured fire from her soul, Laurel said on a caustic note, 'Exciting but dangerous.'

'Just the worst sort,' her mother agreed gloomily. 'Still, darling, you didn't have time to really fall for him, did you?'

'Good heavens, no!' Only enough time for him to make all other men seem tame, dull and totally lacking in the sexual charisma he exuded.

And, if her negative was a little too emphatic, her mother didn't seem to notice, enquiring instead, 'So, have you decided to go to Sarah's party tonight?'

'I suppose so.'

'It will do you good,' her mother said bracingly. 'Stop you moping, and turn your mind to other things. Sarah's parties are always a bit wild—just what you need. You've settled into a rut, darling.'

Wildness? Was that why Alick had appealed so much to her?

No, he wasn't wild; that was just her imagination. He was a flirt and a cheat, and for a little while he had wanted her so much that she had been able to taste his desire, breathe it in, feel it setting light to her inhibitions and fears—and she was not going to let him into her mind again!

Clad once more in her basic good silk, she decided yet again that the first thing she was going to do when she had a job with a decent salary was to buy some clothes. When she had made up, she stood for a moment looking at herself. But she saw nothing new, merely a small, slightly too voluptuous woman whose nagging restlessness showed in the unquiet glitter of topaz eyes and the soft disciplined line of her mouth.

'Stop being so stupid,' she muttered through clenched teeth as she turned to go.

This intolerable sensation of being lost in a dark unknown land without a compass or guiding star was only temporary. It was just that she had almost achieved the goal she had set herself when she left Martin: first, to finish her arts degree, then, to get a Masters, and naturally she was feeling a little let-down. It had been her lifeline. Oh, she had loved university, relished the expansion of her horizons, the new disciplines and ambitions, enjoyed her work with students; but the most important thing had been the slow return of the self-respect and confidence that Martin had stripped from her.

Well, most of it. She was still too fragile where her sensuality was concerned to risk putting it to the test. Common sense told her that her failure to respond had not been all her fault, that Martin's greedy lust had had some part to play in it; but in this case common sense couldn't prevail against her memories of the jeers and insults she had endured during her year with him, and the revulsion she had felt when he made love to her.

Perhaps, she thought, her skin heating at the memory of Alick's avid mouth and her equally avid response, perhaps time too was working its magic in that aspect of her life. It wasn't revulsion she had felt when she lay twisting and turning on the bed in Alick's arms.

But then she thought of the inevitable outcome of such caresses, the humiliating helplessness, the exposure, and her flesh crawled. No, she would never be ready for that.

It had been a long, slow struggle back to self-esteem, but she had made it. Until three weeks ago she had been totally satisfied with her life, and she was not going to let another arrogant male reduce her to the pathetic creature she had become by the time she had summoned up the strength of mind to call an end to her marriage.

Surely these past years had taught her something! Something more than the fact that, due to some spiteful quirk of fate, she was vulnerable to a certain physical type of masculinity.

Masochism, she told her reflection; that's what it is, and the sooner you forget it the better.

For once Sarah's party seemed almost staid, the party-goers restrained. 'Post-stock-market crash,' she confided airily. 'I'm entering a sober phase.'

'Sarah, the stock-market crash happened four years ago!'

Her friend shrugged. 'So, I'm a little behind the times; who cares? I am hearing very nice things about your thesis. A little bird whispered to me that it is not boring! Are you sure you want to be a historian, Laurel? If you do, you have to be boring; it goes with the territory. That's why historians have such lethal feuds; they have to put some spice into their lives.'

Laurel grinned affectionately at her. 'Philistine!'

'Admit it! Have you ever heard of mathematicians indulging in battles to the death? Historians do it all the time.' Her voice dropped into reverence. 'Do you know who's here tonight? Alexa Severn Venetos!'

'Really?'

Laurel recognised the name, as would all of Sarah's friends. The woman had been Sarah's mentor and example for years; brilliant, beautiful Alexa Severn Venetos, famous before she was thirty. Now married to an extraordinarily exciting man she managed to combine marriage, children, and her work with what seemed to be enviable ease.

'How exciting for you!' Laurel said, wondering what the woman's system was. Nannies and housekeepers, she supposed; and a rich, doting husband no doubt helped.

'Yes. Her work on the chaos theory——'

'Spare me the eulogy! I read her book about the chaos theory after a reviewer said that "it made a complex and difficult subject simple enough for the layman to understand". I got lost at the end of the first page.'

'Yes, but you're a historian!' Sarah grinned. 'No brains at all, merely re-digesting material that's already old! No, Laurel, you're not allowed to hit me at my own party! Come and meet Alexa, she's an absolute darling and she'll be nice to you even if you are a historian.'

But, as Sarah pushed through the crowd of people towards a tall black-haired woman, Laurel drew a sudden impeded breath, because talking to Alexa Venetos was a man she recognised.

'My other star,' Sarah muttered from the corner of her mouth. 'Absolutely *gorgeous*, isn't he? Comes from Kerikeri but spends a fair amount of his time jetting around the——'

'He's my cousin.' Thank heavens her voice sounded normal enough.

'Really?' Sarah's astounded and envious look had time to promise an inquisition later, before she abandoned it for one of her stunning smiles. 'Alexa, this is Laurel Webster, who is my very best friend, as well as being Alick's cousin, so I've just heard!'

'First cousin once removed,' Alick corrected suavely.

Laurel's head came up. Her eyes flashed as they locked with the mocking steel-gleam of his. 'Hardly related at all,' she agreed on a savage note.

'Well, not close enough to worry about,' Alick said urbanely, taking her hand to kiss the palm.

Hot colour streaked along her cheekbones as the touch of his lips sent sensations rioting through her. She managed to quell her first instinct to snatch her hand away, and even summoned up the composure to smile sunnily up into his face and say with a sweetness so profound it dripped menace, 'How's Jenna?'

His answering smile was bland. 'Fine,' he said evenly.

And Alexa Severn Venetos, who clearly sensed some of the undercurrents, looked with a startled amusement from one face to the other before interposing, 'I thought only Leon could get away with such flagrantly romantic gestures, but I see I was wrong. Are you sure you haven't a smattering of Italian blood in you, Alick?'

'As far as I know, it's Scottish or English all the way back,' he told her cheerfully. 'Norse Highland Scottish with more than a few bloodstained Vikings, at that. From what I've heard of them, about the last thing you could accuse them of being was romantic.'

He still had Laurel's hand imprisoned in his, his lean fingers forming a cage around hers as she tried unsuccessfully to tug free. When she finally gave up and let them lie resistlessly, he looked down at her, his narrowed gaze a mocking challenge.

'Oh, I don't know.' Alexa's eyes lingered on their hands, her smile oddly sympathetic. 'Romance isn't a matter of bloodlines, you know.'

He lifted his brows at her, teasing her with the intimacy of old friends. 'Really? I know that Leon fell for you like a ton of bricks, but surely mathematicians, especially world-famous ones, are immune to the grosser feelings of we lesser people?'

Alexa's beautiful face melted into laughter. 'What nonsense you talk,' she teased. 'Are you accusing me of marrying Leon for his money?'

Something softened in his expression. 'No, I know why you married him,' he said gently.

She smiled with misty affection at him. 'Yes,' she said with simple frankness. Then she turned her head to the two women who were watching this piece of by-play with unhidden interest. 'Alick and I have known each other since we were children,' she explained cheerfully. 'We're old friends and old enemies. Alick pulled my hair when we were both five and then rescued me from the top of a tree when I couldn't climb down.' She grinned. 'Of course, he was the one who dared me to climb there in the first place. Alick, why don't you take Laurel somewhere where you can dance, so that Sarah and I can exchange a few technicalities?'

She got away with such blatant manoeuvring, too; besides being beautiful she had, Laurel thought wearily, some of Alick's charm and ability to manipulate people.

Most emphatically, she did not want to obey. She remembered only too well what had happened the last time she had danced with him, and there was no way she was going to risk a repeat of that conflagration.

However the hand clasping hers urged her into the next room, where bodies were gyrating in the semi-gloom. Sarah always insisted on the noise level being kept down far enough to allow conversation, but even so there were too many people in too small a space.

'I don't want to dance with you,' she hissed as loudly as she dared.

'I'm not sure that I want to dance with you, either, but I'm not going to be too pointed about it,' he said in a hatefully reasonable tone. 'Five minutes should see us through.'

'Five minutes——'

But her protest was lost as he jerked her into his arms and commanded savagely, 'Just shut up, will you?'

Of course, the music chose just that moment to turn slow and sensuous. Of course. And there were so many people dancing in such a small space that she was, perforce, pressed against the leanly powerful length of his body.

Gritting her teeth, she determined that this time she would resist the blandishments of her weakness. She strove to recall Martin, his handsome face contorted into malevolence as he flung insults at her.

But the nightmare refused to come, blanked out by her response to the man who held her not too close, his expression aloof while his body promised her hidden, subliminal, forbidden delights.

As it appeared that she was attracted to men with lean, rangy bodies and dark blond hair, perhaps, she thought with a small cynical twist of her lips, it had just been her bad luck that she had met Martin, with his mean spirit and his scorn for all that she held worthwhile, before she met Alick.

But was not Alick as bad, engaged to one woman, flirting with another?

Except that the word 'flirting' had connotations of light frivolity, of cheerful wit and casual lovemaking that bore no resemblance to the violent hunger that ached through her whenever she saw him...or thought of him, she admitted wearily.

And the moments they had shared in her bedroom at Kerikeri had been about as far removed from flirtatious as anything could be. There had been a driven intensity to their lovemaking that even now had the power to make a pang of need pierce her.

As he turned to avoid a couple who were gyrating barely on the right side of decency, his arm tightened around her. She followed his movements as though she had been born to do it, relaxing against him. He didn't speak, which was just as well because her mouth was suddenly too dry to answer. He was warm against her, his shoulders wide enough to block out everyone else on the floor, so that in this crowded room she felt alone with him. He smelt faintly of male, an erotically masculine scent that sharpened her senses unbearably.

Alert, yet oddly drowsy, every cell in her body suffused with a slow tide of heat, she listened dreamily to the disquieting thump of his heart. The smooth flexion of powerful muscles beneath his well-cut clothes made her swallow, prohibited fantasies of desire and submission shimmering like mirages in her overheated brain.

No! Instinctively she stiffened, but his arm was merciless, holding her against him. She said incoherently, 'I can't—I won't——'

'It's too bloody late.' Anger jagged through the words, but that basic emotion was overlaid by another, a stark unbidden hunger that set her nerves afire.

CHAPTER FOUR

DESPERATELY, Laurel looked up, then froze, her hunted gaze captured by Alick's.

'Fate,' he said with bitter resignation. 'I never used to believe in fate. Never. I was master of my own destiny; I knew where I was going and what I wanted so I took steps to see that I got there, and I made it. And now my whole bloody life has blown up in my face.'

'Jenna,' she said urgently, using the name as a talisman to deflect him from saying words she should not hear, words that would change her life.

'Yes, Jenna.' His voice was heavy, raw with self-disgust. 'I thought she was part of what I wanted. So I decided to marry her because she's sweet and gentle and intelligent, and because she loves me.'

She bit her lip, holding the words back, fighting them, but they sprang forth, quick, fatally revealing. 'Are you lovers?'

'What do you think?'

It hurt, like a betrayal. Of course they were lovers—they were engaged. The pain sawed through her, savaging her emotions, her deepest thoughts, so that she could hardly breathe with it.

But she had to try because she didn't think she could live with herself if she let this go on. Grasping frantically for objectivity, she said, 'Alick, we can't do anything about this. You are engaged and——'

'And I can't even look at you without wanting you.' He gave a savage, reckless laugh. 'God, who am I trying to fool? I can't even think of you without getting hard. I dream of you every night and every dream ends in your surrender, your mouth ravenous beneath mine, your eyes pleading for me to bury myself in your beautiful body

81

and bind you to me with chains so strong that you'll never leave my bed again, your sweet husky voice moaning as I take you and go with you to whatever forbidden heaven exists for witches and the men they enslave.'

Wildfire ran through her body, setting it alight. She tried to banish it with pain, sinking her teeth into her lower lip until the blood came. But the deep rasp of his words lingered, robbing her of strength and will-power.

Alick bent, and with sensual expertise his mouth touched hers, his tongue soothing the ravaged flesh. 'I want you so much I can't even call myself a man any longer,' he said harshly as he straightened, 'but I wasn't going to give in to this obsession. I have made Jenna promises, and I intended to keep them. I thought I had the strength to do that, even if I was unfaithful to her in my mind. Then I looked across the room tonight and saw you coming towards me, and the hunger was like a kick in the gut. Because, promise or no promise, I can't control whatever it is that I feel for you. It's a kind of madness, eating into my honour, infecting my whole life.'

Made guiltily furious by this dismissal of the destructive attraction between them, yet aware in some deep part of her that behind his contempt there was anguish, she said icily, 'Madness describes it exactly, you know. Some stupid quirk of nature, some reason hidden so deep in my subconscious that I can't track it down.'

'What are you talking about?'

She gave a hard, bitter little laugh. 'Oh, did you think I'd fallen in love with you? Sorry, but it's just as physical for me as it is for you. Sex, that's all. For some obscure, benighted reason I respond to men who are about six feet two tall and have hair the same colour as yours, and who walk with that easy smooth stride. Just like you. And Martin. The man I married, if you remember.'

There was a moment of silence during which she was certain she could hear the cells in her body humming.

Then, 'So that's what it is.' His voice was silkily soft. 'How inconvenient for you, Laurel. Tell me, do all men who look like me have to throw you out of their beds?'

His crudity hit her like a blow. She said icily, 'No, and neither did he, nor you.' A quick twist freed her; she looked him up and down with as much scorn as she could summon then finished, 'Let fate off the hook, Alick. I don't suppose we'll see each other again.'

She didn't look behind her as she walked stiffly from the room, but she felt his stare right down to the soles of her feet. Fortunately Sarah was still busy with Alexa Venetos, so Laurel was able to get out of the door without any fuss.

It was warm, one of Auckland's sticky nights, and as she ran to the gate she shivered, feeling the humidity press down on her. A round moon floated muzzily in a sky filmed by high, thin cloud; the air tasted secondhand in her parched mouth. Hurrying across the road to where she had left her car in the shadow of a magnolia tree, she pulled out her keys.

But as she went to unlock the door a hand came from behind and closed over hers, holding it still. She knew who it was; even as her brain demanded to know how he had managed to get there so silently her mouth was shaping his name.

'Let me go, please,' she said, trying to sound authoritative and impersonal.

He laughed. The hair stirred on the back of her neck, but before she could speak he said lazily, 'You made a mistake when you ran away. Fleeing prey rouses the predator, and you are such desirable prey, Laurel, soft and tender and sweet, with enough tang in you to make a tasty morsel.'

Threatened by the implacable note in his voice, she stiffened. 'Don't be silly,' she said in her best brisk, schoolmistressy voice, fighting a potent amalgam of anticipation and anger leavened by an unknown fear.

'Silly? Is that what you used to say to your poor fool of a husband when he told you how much he wanted you? Did you slap him down in that short, sharp, school-prefect's tone?'

'Leave Martin out of this.'

'You brought him in,' he told her unanswerably. His fingers tightened; he turned her with inexorable strength and the next moment she was locked against him, and all hell broke loose as they kissed, open mouth pressed to open mouth, her hands slowly sliding up to encircle his neck, hard-muscled arms holding her captive against his supple body.

Desire burned as it had the last time they kissed, only now her hunger was sharpened by abstinence, fed by time, and she strained to be closer, to lose herself in the passion building up inside her to an unattainable climax.

Through the miasma of sensation her brain struggled desperately to remind her that she had experienced passion before; she had wanted Martin—but when it had come to the crunch she had been unable to follow through.

Yet there was a difference, only she couldn't work out what it was because the fumes of need clouded her brain.

'What is it?' He had lifted his head and was looking down at her, a glittering sliver of colour barely showing beneath each weighted lid.

Her mouth was stiff and tender as she whispered, 'No! Can't I get it into your head that I don't want this?'

'Oh, I believe that intellectually you don't, but your body is demanding it.'

'I'm not just my body,' she hissed.

'Of course you are; at the moment, anyway. You've just told me so—that any man who looks and walks like me and your ex-husband attracts you. That, my dear, is nothing but lust, the carnal desire for a physical relationship, where logic and honour and emotion have no place.'

As if to punish her he kissed her again, and this time there was no tenderness at all, just a bruising forcefulness that for some strange reason set her on fire. When Martin had insisted on his rights and backed his demands by force he had only served to increase her repugnance; but Alick's brutality called forth a savage, primeval response.

She moaned softly in her throat and instantly the kiss gentled. 'I'm sorry,' he whispered against her mouth. 'God, you drive me mad. Open your mouth for me, Laurel. Open it, I want to taste you properly.'

Without volition, her lips parted in an unconscious signal that he acted on immediately. She groaned again as his tongue explored her mouth in a mimicry of the most intimate embrace of all. His arms tightened; she realised how strong he was when he pulled her off her feet and into his aroused body, holding her cradled against him.

Heat gathered deep inside her, coalesced at the fork of her body; heat and fire and a pointed need that made her gasp and wrench her face away and push at him with hands that scrabbled fiercely against the tense width of his chest.

'No,' she said, half sobbing. 'No! Leave me alone!'

He slid her down his body, his mouth twisting in a fierce feral smile as she flinched at the unmistakable signs of his arousal. Shuddering with the effort, she wriggled lithely free, away from the aggression and anger she felt in him, away from her own antagonism and the fiery need that held them both in thrall.

She wanted nothing more than to get back into her car and drive away from him, never to see him again; but he said scornfully, 'And how do I compare with your husband? Poor bastard, did he ever learn that it was just his looks that turned on all that sweet fire, that any man with fair hair and a certain type of body could have you? He must have; presumably that's why he left you.'

Her hand connected with his cheek, the stinging force unfelt by either of them, although he had jerked his head back swiftly enough to avoid most of the blow. She hissed through white lips, 'You are just as much a bastard as he was!'

She thought he was going to hit her back, but a taut moment after she watched his hands clench into naked fists he mastered the fury her impulsive blow had unleashed. The lean fingers slowly relaxed.

'So now we know where we are,' he said with a curious flat finality that frightened her even more. 'Hooked on physical attributes. Oh, don't look so afraid, I'm not going to hit you, however richly you deserve it. Get into your little car and run away again, Laurel; this time I'll let you go. But when the time is right for me, start looking over your shoulder, girl, because I won't be far behind you. There's no place you can run to where I won't be able to find you. And when I do, you lying, sensual little bitch, I'll rid myself of this damned itch if it's the last thing I do, purge myself in your flames until I'm sated and there's only disgust left.'

She whitened, her skin cold and prickling with fear, but her mouth tightened as she spat back, 'And then, no doubt, you'll ask forgiveness of your pretty, loyal, kind-hearted Jenna and she'll take you back. I'd rather die, thank you very much, *cousin*.'

Her voice underlined the last word with vicious emphasis. Opening the door of her car she slid in, slamming and locking it with fingers that fumbled in her desperation to be gone.

He made no attempt to stop her, and when she looked for a second in the rear-vision mirror she saw him still standing on the footpath; looming, ominous in the hazy moonlight.

The concentration needed to drive home eased her turmoil a little, but she was still shaking when she opened the front door, and very relieved to discover that her mother had had one of her rare early nights. At least she didn't have to face her until the morning.

She couldn't sleep. Normally she had no difficulty; she had always been able to go to sleep the moment her head touched the pillow, but she huddled in her increasingly uncomfortable bed and watched the lights of the city dim, and the moon dwindle into ineffectuality until it too faded under the grey light of dawn. Keeping time by the chimes of the grandfather clock in the hall, she lay aching and angry, thoughts racing despairingly around her head.

She had to be crazy. Hadn't her experience with Martin taught her anything at all? Why was it that for some deep-seated, probably Freudian, reason she was vulnerable to tall lean men with lithe, loose-limbed bodies?

Of course she didn't fall in love with them; she just wanted them with a lust that, as degrading as it was, seemed to be insurmountable.

And it didn't last. Her wedding night had shown her that. For the first time in years she thought back to that disaster, trying to fathom out why it had all gone wrong. She had wanted Martin so much, yet the moment he had progressed beyond kisses it was as though he had had no right to touch her.

Oh, she had tried. She bit her lip as she thought of her efforts to relax under his lovemaking. But neither then nor at any other time had she been able to accept him as her lover without, in effect, gritting her teeth. He hadn't realised, or not at first; it was only later that he had started calling her frigid, a tease who had promised him everything and delivered nothing.

Why? she wondered, as she had wondered so often and with such despair. What had happened? Was she fatally flawed, a woman who for some deep undiscoverable reason was unable to tap into the vein of sensuality that ran so fiercely through her?

She recalled the panic that had struck her on the morning of her wedding, the realisation that she was tying herself to another human being, a man she knew practically nothing about. Martin had pursued her in a whirlwind courtship, culminating in a wedding only three weeks after they had met, a wedding her father had disapproved of. After the initial expression of that disapproval he had been kindness itself, but she remembered him saying to her, as she stood helpless in the grip of that strange fear, 'Laurel, it's not too late, not even now.'

She had said quickly, in a hard voice she didn't recognise, 'It's all right, it's just bridal jitters. Everyone has them.'

When he had probed further she had snapped at him, and he had desisted; but he had watched her all through the ceremony with concern in his eyes.

Had her subconscious realised, even then, that she was making a mistake?

Her mouth tightened in a futile effort to hold back her emotions. Oh, she was so afraid of passion; it swamped the logical processes of her mind, it made her vulnerable to Martin, to Alick.

It had lured her into that mockery of a marriage. She had tried so hard to make it work, but eventually she had had to leave Martin. He had wanted a docile, sweet wife who would accept him as the head of the family and let him take the lead in lovemaking, a traditional wife. But he hadn't been content with a traditional wife's substitute of duty for passion; no, Martin was modern, he had wanted it all: a wife who combined an obedient acceptance of her position as a second-rate citizen with a passion that never said no.

Unfortunately Laurel hadn't been amenable. So he had tried to turn her into his version of the perfect wife, first of all insisting that she give up her university studies, then sneering at every interest he couldn't share, all the while taunting her because she 'made love like a log of wood'.

Slowly her emotions had changed from the initial horrified bewilderment to a resigned acceptance of her own part in the fiasco that was their marriage. Struggling with her coldness, she had begun to believe Martin when he blamed her, until one day she had looked at his handsome face and perfectly formed body, his sophistication and careless, painful confidence, and she had seen a cruel, petulant child, unable to look beyond the satisfaction of his own desires.

So she had left him, sadly realising that the love she had thought eternal was a snare and a delusion. She had been in love with love.

But Martin couldn't leave it at that. His vision of himself was as a man who didn't make mistakes, whose expertise in sensual games was so great that no woman was able to resist him. He had badgered her almost daily, trying to persuade her to go back to him, aided and abetted by his mother who couldn't understand why any woman would want to leave her perfect son.

Icy chills crawled across Laurel's skin as she remembered those dreadful months, harassed by Martin's demands that she return, and then the trauma of his death, the death for which his mother blamed her. If it hadn't been for her parents' determined support she might have succumbed to Mrs Du Fresne's hysterical denunciations.

It had left her scarred for life. Somewhere along the way she had come to the conclusion that her precious freedom, the liberty to be herself, was too dangerous to risk. She would never marry again.

The passion that flamed into being when she saw Alick only reinforced her convictions. Mindless, cheating, so intense that neither the loss of control nor the treachery to Jenna seemed to matter, it appalled Laurel that neither of them seemed to have any defence against it.

Vowing not to think of him again, not to let him into her mind at all, she spent the next month or so working with ruthless discipline. She marked the examination papers she had set before fine-tuning her thesis until her supervisor said one day, 'Right, that's enough. You're quibbling. I can see no reason why you shouldn't do very well with this; any more work on it will lead to splitting hairs and over-writing. Put it away, and promise me you won't even touch it over the holidays. You're beginning to look all attenuated and colourless. Go away and eat lots and lie on a bench and read a big, fat, juicy novel about murky doings in the jet-set.'

'But——'

'I mean it. If you can't promise me that, you can leave the manuscript here.'

Smiling, Laurel gave in gracefully. 'All right, I'll leave it strictly alone.'

'Good. What are you planning to do for the holidays?'

'I'm not sure.' She shrugged. 'We've always spent Christmas at home, but this time my mother and I might go off somewhere; to a beach perhaps.'

Her supervisor looked at her, reading the sadness in her mobile features at the thought of the holiday season without her father. 'Each anniversary after a death is hard,' she said gently, 'and Christmas doubly so; but, although it's trite, it's also true that time helps. How did you get on with the article you were doing for ATU on their new headquarters building?'

'I've finished it. More to the point, they liked it, and paid me.' She smiled. 'Quite a lot, too.'

'Have you thought of doing any more?'

A little self-consciously, Laurel admitted, 'Yes, I've done a couple of articles for the *Historic Places Trust* magazine, and one for the local paper on the earliest settlement in our suburb. And, amazingly enough, they've all paid, so I'm actually rather well off at the moment.'

Her tutor gave her a thoughtful look. 'Have you ever thought of making your living as a freelance journalist? You have a smooth, easy-to-read style and a good ear for language—handy talents for a journalist, and I think you'd probably enjoy the work. You're good with people, too; quick at picking up on character and attitudes—I've noticed it with your students. Very pertinent comments on some of their papers!'

'Would I be able to make a living?'

'Possibly not at first, but you could fit it in with other jobs. Why not think about it, anyway?'

It was a completely new idea to Laurel, but the more she thought of it the more she liked it. She even went so far as to make a few notes on the possibilities, throwing herself with more energy into the prospect than she might have normally.

It certainly took her mind off her stupidity over Alick. Her interest was reinforced when she managed to sell a short mood piece, describing her favourite beach, to a glossy city magazine for what seemed to be an exorbitant amount of money. Suddenly the prospect of being a journalist stopped being an idea and became a possibility.

On the strength of it, she plundered her scant savings to buy a pair of sandals and some crisp summer dresses. She even found a new bathing-suit, shopping around until she found exactly what she wanted: a bottle-green second skin with a discreetly cut leg-line.

And then she came home one sticky summer afternoon from a tiring day spent with Sarah, who had been intent on spending up to the limit on her credit card, and discovered her mother smiling and waving a letter at her.

'Hello, that looks as though it has good news,' she said, collapsing gracefully into a chair and easing off her shoes.

'It's from Aunt Helen. She wants us to spend Christmas in Kerikeri with them.'

Laurel froze, staring blindly out of the window while her brain raced into top gear. 'And you want to go,' she said at last, speaking as though her mouth were plugged with cotton wool. For the first time since her father had died she heard anticipation in her mother's voice; to keep it there, she would have done almost anything—anything but face Alick again.

'Yes. We haven't spoken of it—it's been too raw—but I haven't been looking forward to this Christmas.'

'I know.' Laurel padded across to her mother and put her arms around her, leaning her cheek against the top of her head. In a steady voice she said, 'I know, Mum. It's going to be hard without him. We'll go to Kerikeri, then. When do they want us there?'

Her mother returned her hug, unable to hide the shimmer of tears in her over-bright eyes. 'Whenever we like, and for as long as we like,' she said joyfully. 'For at least a week beforehand, Aunt Helen says, so we can enjoy the parties, and until after New Year—more parties!'

'It sounds as though it will be great fun,' Laurel said, gently disentangling herself. 'You'll have to buy some new clothes.'

'And my Christmas present to you will be a superb new dress, so you won't have to wear that tired old silk thing all the time!'

Laurel objected, but her mother was determined, and somehow the next day found them both in a very special little boutique in Parnell. There, Laurel let herself be talked into a silky slither of periwinkle and blue-violet which paradoxically emphasised her eyes to brilliantly glowing amber jewels. It was love at first sight, although her fears about the price were reinforced when her mother refused to let her look at the tag, sweeping aside her initial resistance by informing her loftily that it was part of her Christmas present.

Because she was in love with it she allowed herself to be persuaded. Not, she told herself fiercely, because she wanted to look good for—for anyone. She even bought herself a whole new make-up kit.

But when she thought of the holiday season a hollow icy feeling in her stomach vied with a febrile excitement. However, she would be safe; not even Alick would try to proposition her with the woman he was engaged to in residence. And, for herself, propinquity might overcome this obsession, because surely it had fed on distance and strangeness. The more she saw of him the less exciting and forbidden he would become.

Three days before they were due to set off she was sitting in the backyard, reading in the shade of their magnolia tree, when she heard the front doorbell ring. As Maureen was out visiting a friend, Laurel put down her book, a weighty tome on New Zealand history, and with a resigned sigh went to answer the summons.

Her jaw dropped when she saw Jenna standing there, her pretty face set in lines of rigid control.

'Can I come in, please?' the younger woman asked hurriedly, as though she was on the edge of bolting.

'Yes, of course. Please do.' Laurel held the door open, and closed it behind her, turning back to the younger woman with her astonishment under control. 'Come into the sitting-room and I'll get us a drink. It's terribly hot, isn't it?'

A muscle worked in Jenna's slender throat. 'I—yes. Yes, it is.' She touched her tongue to her lips and blurted, 'You must be wondering what I'm doing here.'

'A bit, although school's out for the year, isn't it? Did you come down to do some shopping?'

Jenna flushed. 'That's what I told everyone, but actually I came down to see you.' Her candid blue eyes were tormented, but there was determination in her voice and the lift of her chin.

In spite of the hateful jealousy that crawled through her, Laurel could see why Alick had chosen her to be his wife. She had courage and integrity.

'Well,' she said, after a tense little moment, 'come in and tell me why.'

Jenna didn't even look around the sitting-room; she perched on the edge of a chair and said, so quickly that the words fell over each other, 'I came to ask you not to come up to Kerikeri this Christmas.'

The request was not unexpected. Alick must have given something away. Or perhaps it was the fabled intuition of a woman in love.

Laurel said quietly, 'I'm sorry, but I have to. My mother won't go without me, and she needs this break.' Her voice wavered, then firmed as she went on, 'My father died last February, and Mum has been dreading the thought of a Christmas season with nobody but me to share it. She's over the moon at the thought of meeting her new relatives, and being in Kerikeri will take her mind off the fact that Dad isn't with her. Next year it will be easier.'

Jenna's white teeth sank into her bottom lip. 'Please don't come,' she whispered.

'Believe me, I don't want to go.' Guilt and jealousy and pain reeled together in an unbearable swirl of emotions. In a voice so rigid with control that it probably sounded superior and stiff Laurel added, 'But you don't need to worry. I'm no threat to you.'

Jenna gave a convulsive sob. 'That's what Alick said after the diamond wedding party.'

'What do you mean?'

'Both of you must think I'm stupid. I knew something was happening—no one within twenty feet of either of you could have missed it, in spite of the fact that you both did your best to pretend that everything was normal.' Her mouth turned down. 'You couldn't keep your eyes off each other, and whenever you were within ten feet the air practically scorched up! I couldn't bear it. So I—I asked Alick, and he said there was nothing to worry about. And, because I trusted him, I believed him. But he was—different. Distant. Then a few weeks ago he came back from Auckland and I knew he'd seen you again. He didn't have to tell me anything—I just knew! He was so withdrawn; he looked as though someone had hit him in the stomach and left him winded. I didn't say anything about it this time—I was too frightened, but after that he stopped——' Colour raced up her skin and she shot Laurel a look in which triumph and defiance and pain were equally blended. 'We stopped sleeping together,' she said baldly, and blushed even more deeply.

Laurel closed her eyes, ripped by a pang of jealousy so intense that it was all she could do not to scream and faint with it. Because Jenna seemed to expect some answer, she said through gritted teeth, 'I don't think you should be telling me this, Jenna.'

'Why not?' She showed her teeth. 'Because you don't like to hear that while he was sleeping with you he was making love to me?'

'That would make him a cad,' Laurel pointed out. 'And I'm sure you couldn't love a cad. Alick and I have not slept together, not ever.'

'Then it's only a matter of time,' Jenna wailed miserably. 'Oh, God, why can't you stay away? I love him so much, and you don't, do you?'

Oh, she was not stupid. Laurel drew a ragged breath, hating the pain that shot through her. She said slowly, 'What I feel is not important. Alick——'

'You mean that it's none of my business! But it is, it is! You're ruining my life, just as you ruined your husband's life, just as you'd ruin Alick's life. He doesn't need a woman like you, a sexy man-eater; he needs someone who will understand him, make a home for him, look after him and love him.'

At the reference to Martin, Laurel went white, but she retained enough composure to say crisply, 'I understand how you feel, but——'

'How can you?' Jenna's face crumpled. With a despairing gasp she whimpered, 'I love him so much, I can't bear it... Oh, I knew it was impossible, I knew you'd only laugh at me——'

'Look,' Laurel interrupted in her turn, heartsick but a little nettled, 'I'm not laughing, believe me, and I feel incredibly sorry for you, but there is nothing I can do. I've seen Alick only once since the diamond wedding, and that was purely coincidental. I'm truly sorry if you're having problems, but I don't see how you can expect me to do anything about it. You seem to see me as some sort of *femme fatale*, but I assure you that I am not. And I have no influence on Alick, either.'

Jenna was really crying by now, scrubbing at her pretty face with a sensible handkerchief. 'I knew it,' she wept, 'I knew it was no use, but I had to try. You could have any man you wanted. Why did you have to pick Alick?'

'I did not *pick* Alick.' Each word was delivered through clenched teeth. Sorry though she was for the girl, and racked by her own guilt, she was not going to sit there and be made to feel like some vampire swooping down on any hapless male she fancied.

If the whole scene hadn't been so embarrassing she might have found the notion of Alick being 'picked' extremely amusing. He was very much his own man; Jenna would do well to curb her possessiveness. If she didn't understand Alick's character better than that, she was certainly not the right person to marry him.

Laurel tried again. 'I'll get you a cup of tea——'

'No!' The wretched girl bolted for the door as though Laurel had offered to poison her.

'Don't be tiresome.' Laurel heard the exasperation in her voice, and tried to moderate her tone towards the sweetly reasonable. 'You can't go out into the street bawling your eyes out. How did you get here?'

'I came in a taxi,' she hiccuped.

'Then let me get you another one to take you back.'

After a suspicious stare, Jenna capitulated. 'All right,' she said, suddenly sullen.

So Laurel made her a cup of tea and called a taxi, showed her where to mop up, and when the cab arrived put her in it, reflecting savagely that, if Alick didn't make up his mind soon, not only Jenna would be a cot case.

She had recovered some of her composure by the time her mother came home, but she went to bed early that night, and lay for hours wondering whether Alick had decided to call off his engagement.

Jenna's histrionics had touched her. No matter that the younger woman obviously considered her to be a blood sister to Mata Hari, there could be no doubt that she was hurting. Understandably so; any woman who had shared Alick's bed would certainly suffer when he decided the time had come to call things off. If he was anything as good a lover as her instincts told her, then he was superb.

And, ruthlessly crushing an interesting and altogether too seductive fantasy, she began to worry once more about Jenna, her anxiety coloured by an intolerable guilt, her brain going round and round until she at last sank into a sleep that was as disturbed as it was unrefreshing.

The next day, impelled by Jenna's misery, she tested the waters about staying in Auckland for Christmas, but Mrs Webster's response was every bit as dismayed as she had foreseen, and, without further effort or any attempt at explanation, Laurel capitulated. Her first loyalty was to her mother.

And, in spite of the fact that she expected the two weeks' holiday to be a refined form of torture, she knew she would go with her.

Not that Jenna had any need to worry. Laurel vowed that she would make sure she saw as little of Alick as possible, and, as it was clear that he resented this merciless desire as much as she did, it shouldn't be too hard to keep out of his way.

It had been several years since Mrs Webster had travelled north of Auckland, so she was kept busy on the long trip with exclamations and small sounds of recognition.

'I don't know why we don't come up here more often,' she sighed regretfully. 'I'd forgotten how beautiful it is. And I've never been to Kerikeri. What's it like?'

'Small, busy, prosperous. The orchards are tucked away behind hedges so you don't see much of them.

When I came up before, the air was permeated with the perfume of orange blossom. It reminded me of that scent you used to wear when I was little.'

'I remember.' Mrs Webster sighed. 'So long ago, wasn't it? Your father used to buy it for me.'

She fell into an abstracted silence, but this time it was no longer heavy with pain and grief and unspoken fear. Time, as everyone kept saying it would, was working its healing. Later, when she resumed chatting, it was in her normal, bright tones. For all the foreboding that lay like a weight on her heart, Laurel knew that she had done the right thing for her mother in coming up here.

They arrived an hour or so after lunch to a welcome that was genuinely warm. Great-Aunt Helen looked a little more tired than she had in October, but she brushed it off with a brisk reference to the heat, adding with a smile that her husband enjoyed the hot weather and hated the cold, so one of them was always comfortable.

Throughout the greetings and the cup of tea that followed, Laurel kept an unobtrusive eye on her mother, only moderating the loving surveillance when she saw that Mrs Webster's enjoyment was patently real. She herself was unable to relax. With a spine as straight as a ramrod, she sat in the chair and pretended to listen to the conversation around her, while her ears were straining to hear another, deeper, more resonant voice.

It didn't come; instead, someone dropped his name into the conversation. Carefully she set her cup and saucer down so that the fine tremble in her hand wasn't obvious.

'...Alick will be over for dinner,' Sophie was saying with complacent satisfaction. 'Dear boy; we're all walking rather gingerly around him. I don't know what's the matter, but he's been in a black temper for months now, it seems. And we're very much afraid it may have something to do with his engagement. Jenna does not appear to be happy either.'

Mrs Webster said quietly, without glancing at her daughter, 'I'm sorry if that's so, although I always think that an engagement can be broken with much less strain and trauma than a marriage.'

'Yes, of course, but Jenna is so sweet, so right for Alick!'

His grandmother said bluntly, 'Do you really think so? She's a darling, but she'd turn him into a domestic tyrant in no time flat.'

'Mother! Alick's not like that!'

Old Mrs Forsythe said, with grim humour, 'He's a dominating, tough, uncompromising autocrat, and the only reason we don't see more of that side of him is because he loves us, and we're all willing slaves to his charm. Which is bad enough for his character. Jenna adores the ground he walks on and she'd let him walk all over her, too, which would be inconceivably worse!'

'But he loves her too,' Sophie protested, clearly considerably disconcerted by her mother's bluntness.

Mrs Forsythe shrugged. 'Of course he does. We all do. She's an eminently lovable girl. *I* think Alick's just discovering that loving someone is not necessarily the same as being in love. And, if that's so, then when he chooses next time I hope it's a woman who will give him as good as she gets. Jenna has never really understood him; hero-worship precludes any in-depth study of the hero's character. But Alick does not have a sunny, sweet temperament and neither is he easy to understand. He's a very complex man, and rather a difficult one. And he could make life absolute hell for himself and his wife if she didn't stand up for herself.'

Sophie said blankly, 'I thought you were happy with the match.'

'I wanted Alick to be happy,' his grandmother said with simple directness. 'If that meant Jenna, then of course I was satisfied with her. But she doesn't seem to know how to help him through this bad patch, does she? And there will be other bad patches. Alick has always

seemed to be indomitable but he's a human being like
the rest of us; he needs support. If Jenna can't—or
won't—give it, if she is afraid of the thought of him
being vulnerable too, then she is not going to be good
for him.'

She looked directly at Laurel and her mother, both of
whom were feeling a little uncomfortable at this surprisingly frank exchange. 'I'm sorry, but it is perhaps
better that you should know that things are not entirely
settled here. We all rely on Alick far too much, and when
he is at odds with himself, as I suspect he is now, we
worry.'

'Of course you do,' Mrs Webster hastened to say. This
time she did look at Laurel, noting the set expression
and remote eyes. 'Families are wonderful, aren't they?
They help when it's possible.'

Laurel's face relaxed into warm appreciation. Smiling
at her mother, she said pertly, 'And give advice when
it's not.'

Her humour robbed the little observation of any sting,
and in the subsequent laughter, rueful though some of
it was, Alick and his problems were temporarily put to
one side.

But later, when Laurel stood for a moment inside the
same room she had slept in before, her hands were
clenched so tightly at her sides that the knuckles shone
white. Then, with a shrug that hurt, she put Alick from
her mind while she unpacked efficiently and quietly,
before going along to help her mother.

Maureen was admiring a bowl of Christmas lilies in
her bigger bedroom, smiling with open pleasure at the
exquisite white blooms, her face relaxed as it hadn't been
once since her husband's death.

'No, darling,' she said, when Laurel asked if she could
unpack for her, 'you're too late. A very nice woman—
the housekeeper, Samma—such a funny name, I wonder
if it's short for Samantha?—came up and offered, but

I told her I'd rather do it myself; so it's all done, don't
worry about it. What are you wearing to dinner?'

'The cream silk.'

Her mother grimaced, but nodded. 'Yes. It's rather
boringly suitable, more so than your new one. Save that
for Christmas.' She fiddled with a bloom, tucking it
carefully to one side, then lifted her head to look across
the room at her daughter. 'Tell me to mind my own
business if you like, but was it Alick who was the wrong
man?'

'Yes.' The answer was rough on Laurel's tongue. 'How
did you know? Was I so obvious?'

'No, no one would have known, but I thought Aunt
Helen was, perhaps, a little too forthcoming. You can't
tell me she makes a habit of discussing fairly intimate
family business in front of people who are almost
strangers. So I assumed she was doing it for a reason.
I rather think she was giving you the go-ahead, Laurel.'

Laurel's face ached with the effort it took to remain
serene. 'Do you? Perhaps she was, but I'm afraid it's
no go.'

'Why, darling? Is he the same type of person as
Martin?'

'Lord, no.' Her mother's surprise made her moderate
the sharp anger in her tone. 'Oh, Alick's everything his
grandmother called him, but—he's the man Martin
would have liked to have been, I think. However, he is
engaged to Jenna, and whatever the reason for his bad
temper he seems determined to stay engaged.'

It was a good enough excuse; after all, she could hardly
tell her mother that she was obsessed by his physical type.

'Naturally,' her mother said briskly. 'Clearly you don't
want to talk about it, but remember, darling, that I'm
always willing to listen if things get too much for you.'
Her eyes twinkled. 'And I promise I won't offer advice.'

'I know you won't.' Laurel gave her a beautiful, lu-
minous smile. 'I love you, Mum.'

'And I love you too, darling; never more than this last year when you've overcome all the awful things that have happened, and picked us both up. Now, go and use the new make-up you bought and show everyone just how stunning you are. Remember, it isn't called war-paint for nothing!'

But Laurel didn't feel very confident as she came down the stairs. Through the pleasant strands of conversation in the drawing-room his voice was strong and deep, the rasp in his tones stroking along her nerves like a lick of velvet fire. Desire beat suffocating wings in her throat so that she had to fight back a demoralising urge to turn around and race back up the stairs to the comparative safety of her bedroom.

Only, as she had once discovered, she wasn't safe even there. Taking a deep, steadying breath, she walked calmly and with easy grace into the room.

CHAPTER FIVE

ALICK was thinner. The creases from his cheekbones to his jaw were more deeply engraved, and his mouth had a harder, more disciplined line. And the light in his eyes, that steel-sheen shimmer, was a stabbing punctuation to his words as he spoke to his grandfather.

He was standing side-on to the entrance to the room, but as soon as Laurel reached the door his head swivelled with the alertness of a wild stallion scenting trouble, and as she walked through he came towards her with his supple masculine grace, a mirthless smile creasing his face.

'Hello,' he said softly, his gaze searching her composed countenance.

She smiled coolly at him. 'Hi. How are things?'

It was not how she would have chosen to meet him after that last searing incident, with his family and her mother watching, but at least he wouldn't embarrass her in front of them.

He said quietly, 'I've just told my grandparents that Jenna and I have decided we are not going to marry.'

Her lashes flew up, met cynical understanding and a steady, lambent flame that sent shudders down her spine. She knew she lost colour and hated herself for the wild surge of excitement that swept through her. 'I'm sorry,' she said inadequately.

'Yes, so am I. But you know all about the anguish of breaking up a relationship, don't you?'

Still caught in the enigmatic snare of his eyes, she nodded. 'Yes,' she said sombrely.

'How,' he asked with cool deliberation, 'is the thesis coming on?'

'Finished.'

'Good. You'll be ready for a holiday.'

It was a statement she couldn't take at its surface blandness. Warily she scanned his face, seeing nothing but a smile quirking those hard lips, and the tiny flames, hotter blue in the deep blue of his gaze, as his answering survey roved boldly over her face and the suddenly sensitive length of her throat.

'I think so,' she said cautiously, then, angered by the ridiculous inanity of her words, she asked with an attempt at crispness, 'Have you met my mother?'

'Yes, we've been introduced.' Possibly he discerned the shadow in her gaze because he went on, 'I didn't insult her.'

'You'd better not have,' she muttered, feeling a fool again because of course she didn't think he would subject her mother to the fine edge of antagonism that had been there ever since he had laid eyes on her.

His smile was insolent and lazy, not softening the harshly honed features one bit. 'Come and join the rest,' he said. 'And I'll get you a drink. We decided to open some champagne as it's such a momentous occasion: your mother's first visit to her ancestral home. Would you like some?'

She suffered his hand under her arm, jumping slightly as his thumb moved in a slow caress across the smooth skin inside her elbow. 'Yes, thank you,' she muttered, striving for cool composure and failing dismally.

'Are you feeling tense after your long drive?' he enquired, falsely solicitous, a cruel mockery colouring the words.

'I must be. It was hot, and there were some idiots on the road.'

She smiled at the others, grateful for their presence which should have served to dilute the impact he had on her, his words from that last meeting ringing in her ears. 'There's no place you can run to where I won't be able to find you,' he had promised. And, 'I'll purge myself in your flames until I'm sated and there's only disgust left.'

Cold dismay roiled through her, but she put the memory to one side as she listened to the conversation, helping it along in her quiet way, smiling, polite, keeping her eyes firmly off the tall man who drank champagne and watched her with banked fires beneath his heavy eyelids.

They ate dinner in the large dining-room. The champagne having done its work of loosening the ties of formality, her great-uncle insisted on giving a toast to the two 'reclaimed' members of the family, making a short witty speech that had them all laughing. And she watched with pride as her mother answered it, just as wittily, so obviously happy to be there that Laurel knew once again how right her decision had been.

Without volition her gaze slid sideways to the angular, arrogant profile of the man next to her. He had spoken very little, but as she looked up he caught her gaze and that humourless smile tilted his mouth.

'Happy?' he asked, half beneath his breath.

She tore her eyes away, saying in a stilted tone, 'Yes, of course.'

'Of course,' he repeated, taunting her softly, knowledgeably.

After that she tried to avoid him, but, when the older ones sat down in the conservatory to watch the night come down, he commanded, 'Come for a walk with me.'

'I—no, thank you, I'm—tired,' she said on a burst of inspiration.

'Then a little fresh air is what you need before you go to bed.' His eyes met hers in a direct order.

'Oh, go with him,' his grandmother said airily. 'He's always been one for getting his own way; you may as well give in now as later.'

With a vast reluctance, Laurel yielded. It seemed as though her astute mother had read the situation correctly; Helen Forsythe was not averse to throwing her grandson and his first cousin once removed together.

Silently they walked across the sweetly scented lawn and through the border of shrubs and trees to the orchard. There she paused, looking about her.

'What's the matter?'

'When I came up in the spring, the orange trees were in full bloom and the perfume was astounding. I thought there might still be some.'

'Not now,' he said quietly, 'but there's still the citrus smell, tangy and faintly astringent, from the volatile oil in the leaves.' He plucked a leaf from the nearest tree and crushed it, then held it close to her nostrils. The scent prickled them; although not as instantly appealing as that of the blossoms, it had its own pungent allure.

She took a deep breath, pretending that she wanted to draw the scent into her lungs because she refused to admit that his nearness had the power to stifle her breathing. 'I'm surprised you have so much citrus,' she murmured. 'I thought most of the orchardists had cut out their oranges and replaced them with kiwi fruit.'

His fingers touched the rigid line of her jaw, sending tiny chills through her. 'We have a large block of them a few miles out of the village.'

'I see.' She moved beyond his reach. 'And do you grow anything else?'

'More citrus,' he said, his voice amused as he dropped the crushed leaf and let his hand fall to his side. 'Tangeloes and easy-peel mandarins for the Japanese market; we export them on our own account. We have just planted a block of casimiroas. You might know them better as white sapote.'

'I've never heard of them,' she said, hoping that all he heard in her tone was the kind of sensible interest she should be showing. It was difficult to concentrate when the track of his hand burnt like fire across her skin. 'What are they like?'

'They're distantly related to citrus, I believe, but they have green fruit that looks like a Granny Smith apple, and smooth white flesh that's an exquisite blend of vanilla custard with a hint of pineapple and passionfruit flavours.'

'Sounds delicious,' she said hollowly, her stomach clenching at the unashamed sensuality in his voice. 'I suppose you're always on the lookout for new things to plant?'

'Yes. Horticulture is not the easiest way to earn one's living. To a great extent the crop is completely at the mercy of the weather, so the more different fruit one grows the less likely one is to have a complete crop failure. The original orchardists in Kerikeri began with oranges, after a disastrous foray into passionfruit—disastrous because they were killed by whitefly. In those days they had nothing to kill the pests. When Grandy took over the orchard from our grandmothers' parents, he insisted that the only way to keep our heads above water was to diversify. It wasn't as easy as it sounds; other orchardists were quite content growing citrus, and at that time New Zealanders weren't as sophisticated in their eating habits as they are today. The orchard went through some hard times, but he was one of the first to realise the unusual characteristics of kiwi fruit, the excellent keeping qualities that make it such a superb export fruit, as well as its extraordinarily high Vitamin C content and its subtle taste and eye appeal. We planted our block only a year after the pioneers in Te Puke started theirs.'

Laurel nodded. Some of those far-sighted pioneers had become millionaires.

'I've carried his ideas on,' he told her, speaking freely and without the intolerable tension that had marked their previous conversations. 'We have a large area of macadamia nut trees planted. They do very well here, and the market for them is worldwide and nowhere near satisfied.'

Interested, she began to ask questions, learning in a short time just how complicated his job was. Standing there in the warm summer dusk, with his deep voice telling her of the manifold market forces to be taken into consideration, she realised again that he was as much a big businessman as men in smooth dark suits who worked out of plush offices in Auckland.

'It's fascinating,' she said softly.

His teeth showed white in the cool air. 'Oh, yes. But, in spite of modern technology, the computerised irrigation systems and the chartered cargo flights, we are still gardeners. It would only need another cyclone like Bola or Delila for us to lose considerably.'

She nodded soberly, remembering the tropical cyclones he had named and the destruction they caused throughout the North Island, but especially in the farming and orcharding areas. 'Were you badly affected?'

'The kiwi fruit were. Most of the other crops came through without too much damage, although we lost several trees in the shelter belts.'

'They were bad enough in Auckland,' she said sombrely, 'although we were protected from most of the wind. I hate to think what it must have been like here. And now, with the greenhouse effect, meteorologists are saying it could get worse, that we could be exposed to more and bigger tropical cyclones.'

'I'll believe the greenhouse effect when it's been proven,' he said judicially. 'The latest theory is that the unusual weather we've had lately may be due to the sunspot cycle, and has little or nothing to do with any greenhouse effect. Which is not to say that I disbelieve the prospect of the world heating up. We've been polluting it with fossil fuels and untried chemicals for years; we should definitely be cleaning up our act. At last people are realising that it's up to all of us to do something about it. The ban on fluro-carbons should help to save the ozone layer.'

For five minutes or so they discussed the latest theories like, she thought with a small shock, two reasonable people!

When they fell into silence it was somehow companionable. A small zephyr, scented with the evocative perfume of newly mown grass, caressed her skin, and from somewhere way across the orchard came the sound of a morepork calling to its mate. As the sunset glow faded, stars trembled into sight, huge and much brighter than they were in Auckland, freed from the competition of the city lights. A thin silver scallop of moon lay on its back in the western sky, kept company by a huge star.

'What's that?' she asked when the silence seemed to stretch too long. 'It must be a planet; it's not twinkling like a star.'

He followed her pointing finger. 'Venus, the evening star. It's intriguing to realise that we only ever see it as a crescent; imagine how bright it would be if it appeared in the full.'

'I didn't know that,' she said, staring at the radiant thing with awe. Her voice was soft and wondering. 'It's beautiful, isn't it? But then, everything is beautiful here. We don't have such peace in Auckland.'

'Most people miss the noise and bustle.' He gave a quiet chuckle. 'We've had quite a few guests who couldn't sleep because it was so quiet.'

As if to prove him wrong, a motorbike without a muffler sprang into raucous life, revved a few times, then roared off along the main road. Laurel laughed, and he laughed with her, their glances meeting in the soft cool air in something very like camaraderie.

It was the first time she had ever seen him like this, she thought, and wondered why wariness stole through her like a cold breath from the South Pole. The magic of the moment fled, dissipating in the morass of her wariness.

Her skin pricked and she shivered, and he said solicitously, 'I'd better get you back inside. Even in our hottest months most people need a light jacket at night.'

'But not you,' she said softly and, as she realised with a great shock of panic, provocatively.

Her immediate self-recriminations were forgotten when he laughed and slid his arms around her, holding her in an embrace that was firm without being brutal.

'No,' he said on a note of smooth mockery, looking down into her appalled face. 'Fortunately for me, I have an excellent self-regulating thermal system in my body.'

She should have tried to twist free but it was more than his arms that held her. In the dark insistence of his gaze, of his face, was an elemental summons, one she couldn't refuse. So she watched with dilating eyes as his head descended, and she surrendered her mouth to his gentle kisses with a kind of fatalistic yearning.

'So sweet,' he murmured a long time later. 'Like kissing flowers, warm and drowsy in the summer sun. Laurel . . .'

Leaning her head against the wall of his chest, she listened with dreamy abandon to the thunder of his heart. He was hard and warm, and he smelt of aroused male, a subtle tormenting thread of scent that mingled with the other scents of the evening and drained her will-power away. She touched the swell of muscle in his upper arm, startled when she felt it clench against her curious finger. Catching her bottom lip in her teeth, she snatched her finger away.

'I like your hands on me.' His voice rumbled through his chest.

She looked up, into a face that was drawn and hard with desire. Panic leached the golden glow from her eyes; she pulled away, slowly, cautiously, like a small animal easing out of the range of a predator.

Although he let her go without a word, that far too observant glance remained fixed on to her face. After a moment her breath came more easily, the braced stiffness in her expression relaxing. Alick had looked at her with the untamed appetite of a tiger on the hunt but he had not shown any of Martin's crude determination to force her.

He never had, she thought in astonishment. Oh, he had kissed her against her will, but she had never been threatened as Martin had threatened her during the whole of their marriage. She stared at the impassive face above her, realising with a jolt to the region of her heart that she trusted Alick Forsythe.

'I'd better take you inside,' he said, holding out his hand, palm upwards. 'You're tired.'

Shyly, almost holding her breath, she put her hand in his, feeling sensation run in dazzling streamers up her arm as his hard calloused fingers closed warmly around hers. She was being an absolute fool because, trust-worthy or not, Alick was an exceedingly dangerous man. But just for this once, surrendering to the unusual pleasure of being the one cared for, rather than the carer, Laurel walked hand in hand with him back across the dew-damp lawn to the wide terrace outside the morning-room. It was in darkness, but lights were blooming in the conservatory and the sound of laughter floated from it.

'Do you want me to tell them you've gone to bed?' he asked as they stepped in through the open french windows.

She would have liked that very much, but the good manners her mother had drilled into her made her shake her head.

'No, I'll come and say goodnight.'

No one seemed surprised at her early bedtime, no one asked what had put the stars in her eyes or the dreamy smile on her soft mouth; they smiled, these people who were her closest relatives, and wished her goodnight, and said nothing as she left them and walked up to her room.

The mood of dazed happiness lasted her into the oblivion of sleep, but whether she dreamt badly during the night, or whether the calm common sense she prided herself on had at last been able to assert itself through the sensuous web he had woven around her, she woke in the morning with a feeling of such intense foreboding that she shuddered with it.

How could she have been so stupid as to let her tiredness and the warm summer evening and a few soft words coax her into mindless, submissive acquiescence like that? Sitting up in bed to watch the sun leap over the tall graceful Japanese cedars in the shelter belt, she decided that she would be cool from now on, not stiff, because she thought he might find that provocative; just calmly, pleasantly distant.

And she would not give him any openings as she had done the night before!

No one stirred in the house. Outside the morning called to a deep inner restlessness, and she got up and pulled on a pair of threadbare jeans and a faded T-shirt. For a moment she hesitated; the shirt made the most of her slightly too opulent bosom, but surely nobody was likely to be about at this hour to notice it. With a casual shrug, she slid her feet into old sandshoes and penned a short note to her mother telling her that she was going exploring and would be back by eight, poked it under Mrs Webster's door, then tiptoed down the stairs and let herself out by the back door.

It was a magnificent morning, the air crisp and fresh and pure, the sun pouring down in a golden flood on to the dew-wet grass. Blackbirds hopped across the lawn, tiny olive-green white-eyes hung from the flowers of a nectar-bearing tree, and a small fantail flew in to dart around her, its high-pitched cheeps interrupted only by the swift eagerness with which it fed on the invisible insects she disturbed.

In the flower borders great lilies drooped heads that seemed drunk on dew, their scent floating heavily on the air. She discovered several interesting enclosures, one a stone seat under three weeping cherries that formed

almost a room of greenery around it. When they were
in flower it would be magical to sit and read a book
there, or just contemplate such beauty.

In another quiet area, walled by high clipped hedges,
there was an Italian garden with a long pool where water-
lilies lifted their heads clear of the still clarity beneath
them, and a fountain played, the dewy drifts of its spray
landing like diamonds on the leaves.

Spellbound, she was standing looking down at the exquisite crêpy flowers of a sacred lotus when she sensed
another presence. Like a small animal scenting danger
her head came up and she froze.

'It's all right.'

Alick.

He had meant to be reassuring, but her face was white
as she turned to face him. He wore jeans as old and as
faded as hers, and an equally faded work shirt, and he
had had time to roll the sleeves up to reveal the strong
muscles of his upper arms. The sun summoned rays of
warm amber from his hair and shadowed the hard angles
of his features.

Remember, she told herself. Cool composure. And a
pleasant but distant courtesy. Her heart was thumping
like a wild thing in her breast, but as he came towards
her she summoned up every ounce of poise she possessed and smiled with an aloof welcome.

'Good morning,' she said. 'How did you know where
I was?'

'When you let yourself out of the back door an alarm
rang in my house. When I got here I followed your prints
in the dew easily enough.'

'An alarm?'

His expression mocked her astonishment. 'Yes. Even
in Kerikeri we have burglars. And my grandparents have
treasures in their house that they refuse to hide away in
bank vaults.'

Like the painting by Turner, which had to be worth
an immense amount of money.

He nodded at the comprehension in her face. 'Exactly,' he said drily. 'So the whole house is rigged to an alarm. Now, where do you want to go?'

'I don't want to go anywhere.' She bit her lip at his raised brows, and said, 'I was just—exploring.'

A faint 'put-put-put' floated up from the valley below, soft, almost melodious in the dazzling air. Tilting her head, Laurel looked an enquiry.

He took her hand in his, ignoring the tug she gave, and set off across the grass. 'Come on, I'll show you what it is.'

It would seem to give the simple movement too much importance if she tried to yank free. And it really meant nothing, she decided with a swift glance at his slashing profile. Brought up by his grandmother, Alick had the kind of fundamental, bone-deep courtesy that was un-fashionable just now, the sort that offered an arm to any woman, whatever her age and status. It meant nothing more than an old-fashioned upbringing and an in-herently protective streak.

Thus justifying the hand that nestled in his, she tagged docilely along, senses keenly attuned to the waking day and the man who strode with noiseless grace beside her. He led her away from the gardens and through citrus and tamarillo blocks, down a fairly steep hill. Like her he didn't speak, although she noticed that his eyes missed nothing as he looked around.

Further down the hill a pheasant called, an eminently satisfying noise. Laurel smiled, delighted by the cheerful calls of a variety of birds—the liquid song of a thrush, a blackbird singing operetta from halfway up a tall gum tree. It was as though they were the first people, the only people in a magical world, enchanted by the quiet dawn into a fairy-tale.

At the bottom of the hill they took a narrow pathway through a wide belt of native trees before, to her astonishment, coming out on to a low cliff above a river, lazy and grey-green, where faint drifts of mist rose slowly above the smooth water. Pohutukawas sprawled over the bank, framing the river with their scarlet and crimson brushes, and on the other side there were mangrove trees rising through the silvery water, olive in colour, tropical and mysterious in appearance, their existence denoting that the river was tidal. And coming up the narrow channel between the bank and the mangroves was the source of the noise: a sleek yacht, mast and boom empty of sails, the small engine leaving a tiny furrow in the water.

The helmsman was concentrating, so he didn't see them, but up in the bows a girl of twelve or so peered down into the water. She looked up and waved, grinned when they both waved back, then swiftly resumed her careful study of the channel.

'That yacht draws too much water for them to be able to get up to the Kerikeri Basin except when the tide's full in, as it is now,' Alick explained.

Laurel lifted a dazzled face towards him. 'I didn't know you backed on to the river,' she said. 'It's so beautiful! Oh, look!'

A pure white heron, the graceful kotuku of Maori fame, walked with dainty footsteps from under the mangroves and flew, clumsily until it broke free of the water, and then with consummate grace, across the channel and out of sight.

'I think it must be last year's chick, too young to breed,' Alick said, his eyes following the rare stranger. 'Otherwise it would be down at Okarito Lagoon in the South Island, raising a nestful of youngsters.'

'I've never seen one before. It's so beautiful.' She sighed, suddenly aware that they were standing very close together. As inconspicuously as she could, she stepped away to safety.

Unfortunately as she did so she looked up and caught the merest hint of a smile, faintly taunting, on his hard mouth.

'By the way,' he said evenly, 'we're all going to a carol service down by the Basin tonight. Do you want to come?'

She, who had always so loved carol services, hesitated. Last year she had gone with her parents. 'I don't know,' she said after a moment. 'If Mum feels that she can cope with it, yes, I think it would be a good idea. But if she can't bring herself to go, I feel I should stay with her.'

'I see she relies on you for support.'

There was no note of censure in the deep voice, but she bristled defensively just the same. Careful, she warned herself, snatching back the hot unspoken words. Calmly pleasant, remember?

'Yes,' she said crisply. 'I'm afraid she does. She and Dad were very happy together, great companions. She misses him very much.'

'She may well marry again.'

She nodded, turning a little blindly away from the river. 'I hope she does.'

He said nothing until they were almost back at the house, when he commanded, 'Come and have breakfast with me.'

Her lashes quivered in shock. Without thinking, she said, 'Oh, no, they'll be expecting me——'

'They won't be up yet,' he said drily. 'Unless your mother gets up this early.'

She looked at her watch. Barely seven o'clock. 'Not quite this early,' she said, smiling slightly. Her mother was a night person.

'Samma's not on duty until eight-thirty.'

The housekeeper was a cheerful rotund woman in her late twenties who efficiently juggled looking after a six-year-old son with her job. She lived in her own flat in the house and appeared genuinely attached to her employers, who were certainly fond of both her and Jonathon, her bruiser of a child.

Laurel bit her lip, aware of the empty feeling in her stomach, and made the mistake of looking up. Laughter, warm and only faintly teasing, glimmered in the dark blue eyes; the hard mouth was relaxed into an amused smile. Although the piercing attraction was still there, she felt something else: a kind of companionship, a bonding that was far from physical.

She sent him her rare urchin's grin and nodded. 'What are you going to feed me?'

'An avocado and bacon omelette,' he said promptly. 'Fresh orange juice. Strawberries. And I make excellent coffee.'

'How can I resist a breakfast like that?'

That tenuous, companionable link between them lasted. Like two good friends, they walked back across the rapidly drying grass while all around them the sounds of the awakening world came, muted through the high hedges. A car started up the road and from somewhere a dog's bark was followed by a burst of whistling. But it was still quiet, and still peaceful.

'You're lucky to live here,' she sighed, remembering the noise of the traffic and the low hum of thousands of people around them at home.

'I'm not always here. I travel quite a bit, and there's a flat in Auckland where I spend at least a third of my time.' He looked around, the chiselled contours of his face set in an expression of fierce, elemental satisfaction. 'But this is my home.'

It meant more to him than the comfortable house where she had lived most of her life meant to her. Envious and curious at the same time, she said, 'That sounds very possessive.'

He turned his hooded gaze on to her. A strange little smile curled his mouth. 'I am possessive,' he said calmly. 'I learned early on that Forsythes don't let anything slip through their fingers. What we take for our own, we keep.'

'Bred in the bone?' She allowed a light scoffing note to colour the words because something in the flat statement had disturbed her, sending a sharp atavistic thrill down her backbone.

His smile widened. 'Believe it,' he said softly, his eyes holding hers for a merciless second. 'It's the truth, Laurel. What I have I hold, until I don't need it any more.'

Like Jenna?

'Ah, here we are.'

They had arrived at the manager's compound, the big packing shed silent now, the wide paved area without any cars. A large Alsatian came walking stiffly up to them.

'Prince,' he said, and the dog gave his hand an adoring swipe. 'You'd better go home, boy, it must be time for you to wake the household up.'

'He's not yours?' she said as the big dog turned and trotted off.

'No, he belongs to one of the men who works for us whose house is over behind the hedge.'

He didn't take her in through the front door but walked around to a side entrance that opened into the kitchen, a pleasant area which, though furnished with the latest in equipment, blended with the big room next to it into a smart, country-style space. It was nothing like the fairly formal room where they had danced the night after the diamond wedding celebrations, yet it was clear that the same man owned them. Alick had stamped his complex, enigmatic personality on his house.

Beyond a dining area the quarry tiles flowed into a large, informal sitting area with two comfortable sofas and several easy chairs, one of which was clearly Alick's, as it had beside it a table upon which a newspaper was folded, along with an impressive tome that looked forbiddingly technical.

'This is lovely,' Laurel observed, looking around her with real pleasure.

Bookshelves lined one entire wall, a large old dresser held bright china, and on another wall was a magnificent abstract painting, the glowing greens and golds and blues so redolent of the day outside the window that she could taste the air and smell the summer scents. The furniture was interesting, some new, some old, but all of it comfortable. Her eyes fell on a superb mottled kauri chest being used as a coffee-table, and a large wing-chair, as well as a modern sculpture that should have looked out of place, yet didn't.

The hiss of bacon brought her head around. Walking quickly across to the kitchen she asked, 'Is there anything I can do?'

'Set the table.' He removed the stones from two avocados with a professional flick of an exceedingly large knife. 'And when you've done that dial 03 on automatic and tell Samma you're having breakfast here, just in case someone wonders where you are.'

Ten minutes later the meal was ready. Laurel found herself smiling while she ate with delicate greed, and if her enjoyment was dampened a little by the knowledge that Jenna had probably sat exactly where she did, and no doubt been every bit as euphoric about it, she ignored it.

Later, when she was sensible once more, she would consider it an object lesson, she promised herself. For now she would live for this moment, and relish it.

Alick spoke of local affairs, amusing her with a dry indulgence that was surprising; she had not thought of him as tolerant. Interested—by now anything he did was fascinating to her—she asked questions, listening to his views and proffering her own.

In return she told a few stories of undergraduate behaviour, making him laugh, before he capped them with a tale of his activities when he too had been a lowly undergraduate. He used a wry wit that she liked as much as she enjoyed the fact that he was the butt of his story.

He might be arrogant and autocratic, and her body might be swept with honeyed fire at the mere thought of him, but he could take a joke against himself.

When she had demolished her omelette they moved on to international affairs, and she enjoyed that too, relaxing in the warm stream of sunlight with the smell of coffee and bacon in the air, her brain stimulated by his, and discovering, to her renewed surprise, that they shared many views.

He had travelled, and not just as an ordinary tourist; he didn't boast, but clearly he had met many people whose names regularly appeared in the news.

When she taxed him with this he grinned and said tantalisingly, 'I've been overseas a couple of times with trade missions, and I've had to deal with politicians in the work I do for the horticultural producers' boards. Very dull, most of it, negotiating with people who are trying their best to get the better of you! Still, there have been one or two interesting moments.'

She looked at him with respect, intrigued by his casual dismissal of what was clearly a responsible and important aspect of his life.

Her heart jumped painfully. With the sun picking out the adamantine contours of his face in unsparing accuracy, his every flaw should be revealed. But the hard, unhandsome face was more striking than any glamorous film star's. He wore the inner power, the inbuilt characteristics of authority and ruthlessness, there for everyone to see.

This man was her enemy; he represented all that she feared, the subjugation of the logical processes of her brain to wild, unrestrained instincts. If she let him get close she could well be so severely burned that she would never recover.

Her marriage had been so painful that even now it was too raw for her to talk about. She thought, a little wildly, that an affair with Alick would finish her off. He would be like Martin, at first incredulous when the passion she had professed didn't translate into action, and then would come the contempt. But no, she thought painfully, Alick would not scorn her for a flaw that was not of her own making. Perhaps, instead of scorn, he would feel sorry for her. Humiliation chilled her skin as she considered that prospect. Martin had wounded her, but if Alick ever looked at her with cold pity she would die.

Suddenly she could no longer bear to be there with him. Putting her coffee-cup down, she said as steadily as she could, 'I'd better get back and let you get to work.'

'I have only a bit of paperwork to do today. I'll walk you over.'

She made the mistake of looking up, to catch him watching her with an amused, ironic gleam in his eyes as though he perfectly understood her sudden desire to get away, but had no intention of pandering to it.

'Thank you,' she said crisply, refusing to show any recognition of his attitude or her reaction to it.

'Just wait for a moment or two while I put the answerphone on and check out a couple of books I want to take back to Grandy.'

'What about the dishes?'

'Do you know how to load a dishwasher?'

She nodded, and he showed her where his was. But, although she took her time about clearing every evidence of breakfast away, he still hadn't emerged when she had finished and she could faintly hear his voice from the hall. On the telephone, no doubt. She wandered out on to the wide terrace and from thence to the wooden sitting-out place by the tiny waterfall.

Beneath a canopy of white summer jasmine, dark green cushions contrasted pleasantly with the subdued grey-fawn of the wood. Water fell with a gentle susurration over rounded volcanic boulders into a pool where a sacred lotus flowered, the pink petals neatly disposed around what looked to be a small golden pepperpot. Fascinated, Laurel sank down on to the cushions, enjoying the sweet summery scent of the jasmine blending with the perfumes from several gardenia bushes smothered in flowers, and the cool freshness of the water.

A large monarch butterfly hovered over the water before settling on a sunlit rock to slowly exercise its orange and black wings, presumably while it pondered the meaning of life.

Slowly leaning forwards, Laurel held out her hand, and to her delight the butterfly flapped the six inches or so and alighted like a brilliant fairy on her outstretched finger. The thin black legs made barely any impression, light as gossamer. Laurel sat with her eyes fixed on to the glorious, gaudy thing, afraid to move in case she frightened it. The innocent, total trust of the wilding somehow set the seal on a wonderful morning.

After several seconds she felt another presence, and lifted her eyes past the butterfly to meet those, slyly amused, knowing, and rather cynical, of a magnificent porcelain dragon, so well camouflaged in its sleek greens and browns that she had not noticed it until then.

A magnificent expression of the potter's art, splendidly indolent yet with more than a hint of menace in the sleek body, it lay basking on a boulder within inches of the waterfall. It was so lifelike that she felt the hairs on the back of her neck rise.

But of course that was Alick, not the dragon. From the corner of her eye she saw him move towards her. Without speaking he sat down beside her, arranging his long, heavily muscled legs beneath the table. How he had managed to get so close without her hearing, and without disturbing the butterfly, still slowly opening and closing its wings, she didn't know; nor did she question how she sensed his presence.

'Look,' she said softly, her voice very low.

'I'm looking. Do you do snake-charming too? And I'll bet you can call dolphins from the sea.'

She gave a delicious gurgle of laughter and the butterfly flew delicately up from her finger, hesitated for a moment, then settled on to his shoulder. It waited there a second before fluttering on through the sparkling air and out of sight behind the feathery fronds of a clump of papyrus.

Laurel smiled brilliantly, excitement and pleasure sparkling in the golden amber depths of her eyes. 'I wish I could. I feel as though someone has just paid me the most enormous compliment,' she said on a note of sheer joy.

He grinned and extended a hand, helping her to her feet. 'I suppose it's no use my telling you that it's probably just hatched out and is exercising wings that are not yet very strong?'

'Not a bit.'

His fingers curled around hers. 'Then I won't. Twenty or thirty miles away towards Whangaroa harbour there's a tiny bay where the monarchs over-winter. It's quite a sight; millions of them on several huge pohutukawa trees. The best time to see them is June, so if you come up on Queen's Birthday weekend I'll take you up there.'

She stood looking at the strength of his fingers, dark, shocking against her ivory skin, and felt the warmth and the exciting contrast of his strong hands against her softer ones. It seemed that he was expecting any—relationship, for lack of a better word, that eventuated to last for more than a few weeks.

In a voice that trembled a little she said, 'I'd like that.'

'Good,' he said, satisfaction implicit in the deep untroubled voice.

More than anything she wanted him to kiss her. In fact, she thought inanely, her lips were stinging for his kiss, their sensitive surfaces throbbing. However, he did not bend his head, although he didn't release her hand either as together they walked across the sun-warmed grass to the main homestead.

CHAPTER SIX

IN THE end they all went to the carol service—Laurel, her mother and Sophie with Alick in his big Jaguar, Samma the housekeeper driving the older Forsythes' regal but ancient Daimler, her son perched up beside her in the front, her employers ensconced in the back.

It was just on dusk, and the water at the basin was very still, dark and depthless as obsidian beneath the cloudless sky. As though in respect, a gentle hush lay over the river and the hills. Even over the ledge of rock where the river fell into the basin the water whispered rather than churned.

People carrying rugs and babies and smiles were pouring on to the area of grass beside an old verandaed house that had been converted into a restaurant. Everyone knew the Forsythes; it was, Laurel thought, accustomed as she was to being an anonymous member of a crowd and a little uneasy at the unabashed interest she and her mother were causing, all very friendly.

Well aware that the other side of that friendly attention could be gossip, she was glad she had decided to wear a soft silk-look shirt of muted paprika above a cotton skirt of golden apricot, and over it a loose waistcoat in a deeper shade than the shirt, embroidered in a peasant style in golds and purples and greens. Further dramatising the outfit, she had borrowed her mother's fake gold earrings and slender leather sandals. She had created the outfit from bits and pieces she had had for years, and was rather proud of it. It gave her nice but ordinary appearance a little spice, she decided. Gypsyish and ethnic, but restrained.

Gazing around, she realised that she could have worn anything from jeans and a T-shirt to a dress that hinted that she was going on to a party or dinner afterwards.

She hadn't looked directly at Alick when he came to collect them, but she had caught the deep note of satisfaction in his voice as he wished her good evening. It ruffled her. Now she noticed Sophie watching them with a small expectant smile, and immediately the shutters slammed down. The last thing she wanted was for the family to assume that she was going to take Jenna's place.

For several very good reasons. Alick had said nothing about love, not a hint that the unmanageable emotions he felt for her had anything to do with that more gentle sentiment. He wanted to make love to her—that was all he had intimated.

And she? Oh, she wanted it too, but she shrank from admitting it even to herself because she knew that, for her, wanting led to nothing. She had wanted Martin, although not like this, not so that a mere meeting of glances was enough to send a sensuous shudder of delight slithering down her backbone to pool hotly between her thighs.

Martin had been an infatuation, the first man to make her realise the power of those primitive needs imprinted in every warm-blooded animal. Instinctive, undiscerning, the blind urge to perpetuate the genes, her response had been a flashfire of passion based on nothing more than a woman's need for a virile male, and it had died swiftly under his uncaring hands.

Her physical response to Alick was far stronger. Somehow she was so attuned to him that like a cat she sensed his presence with her skin, or perhaps even further in, in her cells, the building blocks of her body. Yet there was more to her hunger than the purely carnal. She wanted to know him in every sense, not just the Biblical, although the mere thought of lying in his arms sent erotic little impulses along every nerve in her body. For a moment she allowed her mind to drift, visualising the magnificent contrasts between them, the inherent male power of him melding with her smoother, sleeker, feminine strength, fighting the age-old duel that ended with two surrenders and two victories.

Only lovemaking hadn't been like that for her. Martin had won, every time, and thought his victory of little worth.

She lowered her head to prevent the bad memories from showing in her face and sat down on the rug between her mother and Sophie, smiling vaguely at the latter's whispered suggestion that she move to sit beside Alick. Balked in the end, Sophie gave up, although she couldn't hide her surprise at Laurel's intransigence.

People passed, stopped to chat, to exchange greetings, to meet the newcomers. As she had at the diamond wedding celebrations, Laurel noticed the variety of accents, from a range of English ones through Dutch and North American, some she couldn't decipher, and a few that were obviously from Asia, through to the broadest of New Zealand twangs.

It was all very pleasant, very informal, although Laurel had the uncomfortable feeling that she was on probation. Did these friends of the Forsythes believe that she was the 'other woman' in Jenna's sad love-story? The thought made her profoundly uncomfortable, dimming the pleasure in her smile.

Fortunately she was able to recall the names of most of the people she had met at the diamond wedding anniversary, and with Sophie providing quiet prompting for the few she had forgotten she had no difficulty in introducing her mother. Mrs Webster sparkled. She had always been gregarious, at her best in company. It was wonderful to see her regain her old interest, a confirmation that whatever the cost to Laurel coming to Kerikeri had been the right thing to do.

However, she was rather glad when the light faded and the last people sat down on their rugs. Stars began to prick through the dove-grey radiance of the sky, and on the still waters of the basin a slender white yacht lay like a bird at rest. The graceful branches of the big gum trees that were such a feature of Kerikeri were etched into the deepening sky.

This time last year her father had been with them, she thought, as tears clotted into a thick ball at the back of her throat. She slid her hand around her mother's and held tight, flinching at the fierce grip she got in return. Grief ached through her. She hadn't realised how painful it was going to be, or she might not have come. For her mother's sake she forced herself to sing all the old favourites, and after a while Maureen joined in. If occasionally both voices quavered, well, there were enough people singing for it not to be noticed.

After the almost unbearable poignancy of the preceding hour it was a relief to break and drink coffee and tea, try the home-made scones and cakes and biscuits that were spread out on a large table, and talk to the cheerful locals and their excited children. Laurel relaxed; it didn't appear that Jenna was there. Guilt ate at her; she had to stop herself from scanning friendly faces for signs of dislike.

Not even the electric lights prevented the silver of the starlight from laying a cloak of peace over the calm water and the old trees, the darkened bulk of the Old Stone Store, standing as it had done for over a hundred and fifty years, and the small house beside it that had been the first European dwelling-place erected in New Zealand.

They represented security in a changing world, as did the church above them on its little knoll, and the water and the stars, eternal and unchanging in the dark vault of the heavens.

Occasionally a car came down the hill opposite, swooped across the bridge and on up their side, but even they seemed to travel more quietly then they did in Auckland.

I could be happy here, Laurel thought suddenly, astounded because she had always considered herself a real urbanite. But there was something about Kerikeri; its cosmopolitan people, the natural beauty of its setting and perhaps the history of the place combined to make a particularly attractive little town.

A star gleamed low in the sky, big and silver. 'Look, Mummy,' a little girl said from a few feet away. 'Oh, look, Mummy, it's the Christmas star!'

Her mother smiled, and explained that no, it was Venus; and above them Laurel's eyes met Alick's, hers soft and warm and regretful, his polished by the light of the stars, oblique and enigmatic.

Afterwards they all lit candles and sang 'Silent Night', and tears welled into her eyes as a sudden fierce pang of grief shot through her. She cast a quick glance sideways to see her mother standing still, the steady flame of her candle lighting up the agonised expression on her face as she fought to control her pain.

Then Alick dropped his arm over Mrs Webster's shoulders and held her lightly. He sang on in a deep pleasant baritone and after a second the older woman's features relaxed, although her eyes still glittered.

Laurel clasped her mother's cold hand; neither of them was able to finish the carol, but both felt the current of love and comfort flowing through their joined hands. And, as it ended, Alick lifted the hand that rested so comfortingly around her mother and gave Laurel's shoulder a quick squeeze before taking his arm away.

Later, when they were back at the homestead, her mother sat in the armchair in her bedroom, watching Laurel's averted face with interest. 'Wasn't it lovely of him? I don't know how he knew that I was just about to break down, but he did. Laurel, when you said he was the wrong man, did you mean because he was engaged?'

Her neck felt oddly stiff as she shook her head. 'No.'

Disappointed, her mother said, 'Tell me it's not my business if you like, but why is he so wrong for you? I like him very much, his family adores him and obviously relies on him a great deal, and everyone we saw tonight clearly had the utmost respect for him. Goodness, in my lifetime I've come across very few men with such a forceful personality, and as for his looks—well, he's got the sort of sex appeal that sizzles.'

'Mum, it's not his looks, nor his sterling character.' Laurel's voice was edged with mockery to hide the raw emotion she could barely hold in check.

'Then tell me what it is. Because you are just as aware of him as he is of you. What is wrong?'

Laurel's mouth lifted in a bitter little smile. 'A variety of things, but one of them is that for me the awareness is about all there is. In other words, to reduce the matter to its most basic form, I'm not very good in bed. And I would say that Alick is very virile, wouldn't you?' She made the statement as flatly as she could, refusing to display her pain and resentment.

Her mother looked startled, then blushed a little before, choosing her words carefully, she answered, 'Yes, I'd say so. You can usually tell, can't you? It's that air of confidence, I suppose. And the excess of what we used to call animal magnetism. But why should you think that you would find it difficult to respond to him? Like that, physically, I mean.'

Without expression Laurel said, 'I thought I loved Martin but I couldn't—I didn't——' Colour heated her cheeks and she stumbled to a stop, humiliation roughening her throat.

There was an odd little silence. Mrs Webster looked down at her hands then drew a deep breath, almost as though bracing herself for a confession.

'You were very young when you married Martin. We didn't know he was so selfish, of course, but I was wrong to encourage you to think in terms of marrying him. It was just that you were the same age as I was when I

married your father, and we were so happy—I hoped
for the same for you, and you both seemed so idyllically
in love.' Her mother's face twisted in distress. 'I'm sorry,
Laurel.'

'Mum, don't be silly.' Laurel squatted down in front
of her, enfolding the nervous hands in her own warm
clasp. They were so fragile, she thought painfully; so
thin and cold. 'Have you been feeling guilty about it all
this time? Don't! You must remember how headstrong
and stroppy I was at that age. I really thought Martin
was a knight in shining armour.'

'Instead he was the dragon,' her mother said
mournfully.

Laurel snorted, her mind racing back to the dragon
that crouched, sleek and powerful, on the rocks on
Alick's waterfall. 'That's granting him too much importance. Martin was just a selfish kid, and, when he
realised that I wasn't going to put him and his welfare
ahead of everything else, he turned nasty—just like a
spoilt brat.'

And, like a spoilt child, when he had turned nasty he
used his cruel tongue to make his point, cutting into her
self-esteem like acid through steel.

'He was more than a spoilt brat,' her mother said
firmly. 'A spoilt brat is not necessarily unkind, and
Martin was. Not that we realised what was going on until
you stopped going to university. I still don't know how
he forced you to do that.'

Laurel gave the thin hands a final squeeze and got up,
pacing across to the window. 'I was so stupid.' She leaned
out, and looked up into the cloudless sky where stars
danced and glittered in a broad swathe of diamonds.

For the first time she acknowledged, 'And I was too
proud to admit that things had gone wrong. I honestly
thought that if you fell in love you got married, and
everything was wonderful afterwards. When it wasn't,
when Martin made it obvious that he really only had
one requirement for his wife, that she minister to his

every need, I thought there was something wrong with me.'

Her mouth sketched a bitter travesty of a smile. 'He said that I had fooled him, I'd promised everything and was giving nothing. After all, I loved him, he loved me; what was there to fight about? And I believed him! So I tried to turn myself into the sort of woman he needed. Don't the magazines say that compromise is essential? Giving up university seemed a small price to pay for the perfect marriage.'

But it hadn't been enough. He had wanted more and more sacrifices from her. And eventually she had begun to realise that he was not prepared to compromise at all. Perhaps his frustration had initially been based on her inability to be the passionate woman he had wanted in his bed, but it had grown until he had become obsessed with making her over into his idea of the perfect wife.

To him she had been nothing more than malleable clay, something he could manipulate and pummel into shape. When she had finally realised that no matter how many sacrifices she made he was never going to be satisfied with her, she had left him.

'He drained away all that lovely bright confidence, and made you so jumpy that you used to watch him all the time in case you said something he could use against you,' her mother said quietly. 'I was so glad when you came home. So glad.'

That bright confidence had been the brash conviction that she knew everything there was to know, but Laurel gave her mother a loving smile. Trust her to see the best in everyone.

'If you were so unsatisfactory a wife to him,' Mrs Webster resumed with a snap, 'why did he want you back?'

Laurel shrugged, her eyes drawn back to the area where Alick's house lay behind a high casuarina hedge.

'I suppose he rather enjoyed having his own whipping-woman,' she said quietly. 'And I don't think anyone had ever rejected him before.'

'Then it was high time someone did,' Maureen retorted trenchantly. 'Of course, I blame his mother. She brought him up to believe that he was humanity's gift to the world, and the fact that he looked like something Michelangelo chiselled didn't help matters. I mean, look at the way he told everyone that he had left you when it was the other way around!' She sniffed. 'And although it was a dreadful tragedy when he was killed, I wasn't really surprised. He was always so reckless, so convinced of his own immortality. Well, the inquest proved that, didn't it? He'd been warned again and again that what he was doing was dangerous, but he just wouldn't listen! And remember how he used to drive? I used to be truly terrified that he'd kill you in an accident. Instead, he killed himself parachuting off a mountain. I felt so sorry for his mother, although that soon disappeared when she wrote you that appalling letter.'

Laurel bit her lip. Phrases of that letter were seared into her brain. 'She was distraught,' she said quietly.

'Possibly, but that doesn't excuse her outrageous behaviour!'

By now thoroughly diverted from the subject she had started on, Mrs Webster rambled on to a résumé of the evening, her delight at being a part of the family very apparent.

At last Laurel left her to go back to her own bedroom. Only Christmas, she thought, as she cleaned her teeth and crawled under the blankets. We have to get through Christmas, and then the first one without Dad will be over, and we can stop dreading it.

But as she lay staring at the ceiling she wondered whether she would be as stiff and unresponsive in bed with Alick as she had been with Martin.

Stop it, she commanded fiercely. Why don't you admit that sex is not for you? Imagine how shattered you'd be if you made love with Alick and found that you couldn't respond to him. You came out of the last entanglement with barely any self-respect; you'd have none at all if Alick found you as frigid as Martin did. Her stomach chilled at the prospect.

Next day the sun shone down brightly, so that even at the breakfast table it was hot, a harbinger of the sweltering day to come.

'We need rain,' Sophie said, frowning into her coffee-cup. 'Alick was saying last night that we'll have to start irrigating today.' She smiled at Laurel's raised brows. 'It's volcanic soil here. Free draining. Wonderful in winter because the orchards don't like wet feet, but a week without rain means that we have to irrigate. We used to take our water from the creeks until the year we pumped one dry. Fortunately the government stepped in and put in two big dams, which provide enough water for all of the orchards, even in a drought.'

'If we ever get a drought again,' Alick's grandfather said wryly. 'These past two years have been the wettest I've ever known.'

It was just polite breakfast conversation, but Laurel listened with great interest because these were the day-to-day realities of Alick's life, and therefore fascinating to her.

'Anyway, it looks as though it will be fine for the workers' party on Tuesday night,' Sophie said. 'The weather report says there's going to be no change for a week or so. I know that Alick can hold a barbecue anywhere, but it would be much nicer if we had a good night for it so we can use his terrace.' She beamed happily at Laurel and her mother. 'It's great fun. We all go, and the workers bring their wives and husbands and children, and they swim in Alick's pool and play tennis; after the food's eaten they usually have a sing-song, and then go home round about ten-thirty or eleven.'

'It sounds great,' Laurel said dutifully.

'And this year you will be there.' Her smile was broad and ingenuous. 'They're all dying to meet you both, of course. And then we have drinks on Christmas Eve here, and our New Year party which is always an enormous, casual affair, great fun too.'

Laurel thought she had managed to conceal her somewhat startled glance at the two oldest members of the group, but Aunt Helen must have seen it, for she chuckled and informed her drily, 'The New Year's party is at Alick's, too, which makes things much easier. Hugh and I go home when we feel tired, and then everyone really lets their hair down.'

It sounded like a very busy social round, especially as there were other parties of various sorts to which they were invited, as well as a dinner or two. Laurel began to wonder whether her three reasonable dresses would be enough. Fortunately most of the events seemed to be casual, so her new summer dresses should see her through those.

Her eyes wandered across to the golden day outside. She had woken early that morning but had stayed in her bedroom, afraid that if she went out again Alick might think she was hoping for his company.

Some time during the night she had decided that she was not going to take any more risks. It was too much like laying her head on the chopping block; the passion that flamed between them was too strong, too unpredictable. She was too afraid to yield to its elemental force and then wake with the taste of ashes in her mouth. Better not to surrender; better to continue on the path she had chosen after the débâcle that had been her marriage. At least that way she would not have to face the humiliation that the exposure of her shortcomings brought with it. It might be cowardly, but it was safe.

And if she felt any regret for the things she was denying herself—companionship, marriage, children—well, she had only to recall Martin's face as he had called her frigid to feel that the balance was in her favour. Her skin crawled as the ugly memories took hold, the cruel words, the crude demands made on her unwilling flesh. She could not go through that again.

That day brought more sun, hotter than it had yet been, and the enervating effect of high humidity. The pace of life slowed down to accommodate the temperature.

After lunch, when the two older Forsythes were having their afternoon rest and Sophie and Mrs Webster were collaborating on a particularly difficult cryptic crossword, Laurel took up her post in the shade of the wisteria, pretending to read but in reality composing excuses for not doing as Sophie suggested—going across to Alick's pool for a swim. The mere thought of appearing in front of him in a bathing-suit made her skin tighten, but she was discovering that, for all her charm, Sophie was like the gentlest of bulldozers, applying soft but inexorable pressure.

The sound of a young, angry voice upraised in frustrated complaint lifted all heads. Sophie put aside the thesaurus she was consulting and observed with a frown, 'That sounds very like——'

Aura hurtled out on to the terrace, saying over her shoulder, 'I don't want to ring them—they know I'm here! I told them what I was going to do!'

She was followed by Alick, hefting a pack in his hand and looking grim.

'Aura, dear, what a lovely surprise!' Sophie got to her feet, smiling to hide her concern. 'Were we expecting you?'

The recalcitrant girl bent a particularly ferocious scowl on everybody. 'No, but I had to come.'

'Oh, dear,' Sophie said with a helpless look at the frowning face of her nephew. 'Have you had another quarrel with your mother?'

Both Mrs Webster and Laurel had risen too, and Laurel said quietly, 'We'll just——'

But Aura broke in hotly. 'You don't need to go, I don't care who hears the sordid details, and you *are* family, after all. No, I have not had a fight with my mother, you can't fight with a jelly. I've had one with the creep.'

Sophie gave a faint gasp of protest, but it was Alick who said curtly, 'Your stepfather has a name. Use it.'

Aura almost ground her teeth but was intimidated enough by the tone of his voice to say savagely, 'Then I have just had a quarrel with Mr Halswell and I refuse to stay there any longer.'

'Why?' Sophie asked with resignation, sinking back into her chair. 'Sit down, love. You don't need to bubble away there like a pot that's going to boil over any minute. Sit down and relax. You make me ten degrees hotter just looking at you, and goodness knows it's hot enough today without that.'

Aura's fury vanished in a wide, disarming grin. 'I do love you two,' she said, adding, with an insouciant kiss on Alick's cheek, 'even when one of you comes over all big brotherly and curt.'

She was clad in a pair of jeans that had seen better days, a thin T-shirt and old tennis shoes, and she looked stunning. Laurel couldn't see why Alick's expression still remained cold and inflexible, especially after that artless embrace.

He said brusquely, 'I want your promise that you'll never hitch-hike again, Aura.'

Ignoring Sophie's dismayed exclamations, Aura flounced across to a chair and hurled herself into it. 'I was perfectly safe,' she maintained sturdily. 'I was very careful who I took a ride with, and besides, I had this.' Fishing in the pack that Alick had dumped beside her she pulled out a singularly vicious knife with a garish yellow plastic handle.

There was an instant outcry from the two older women which Aura ignored, looking a defiant challenge at Alick. His expression didn't change. Instead he held out his hand and, after a moment's hesitation, she put the evil thing in it.

'Now promise,' he said quietly. 'No more hitch-hiking. Ever.'

Aura's lush mouth straightened into a thin line, her expression darkening into mutiny.

Fascinated, Laurel looked from one stubborn face to the other.

'Aura.' Just one word, but there was the flick of a whip in it.

'I'm really very sensible,' she said in a considerably less confident voice. 'Truly, Alick.'

He said nothing, merely held her eyes.

'Oh, damn you, Alick, you bossy swine,' she shouted, colour running up though her clear skin. 'All right, I promise. For heaven's sake, anybody would think I was a total idiot!'

Her capitulation was not unexpected. Laurel thought that it would be a very strong-willed person who could endure Alick's compelling gaze, especially when his mouth had thinned into an inflexible line and the angular contours of his face were set in that forbiddingly stern expression.

It relaxed now, though, into a stunning smile. 'No, just hot-tempered and headstrong,' he said as he bent to give her a swift casual hug. 'You wouldn't want me to spend all my time worrying about you, would you?'

Laurel envied her, even while she wondered how Alick knew that the girl would keep the promise he had extracted from her. Because it was obvious that he had no qualms about the reality of her surrender. But then, she thought, with a quick glance at Aura's glowing face, it was patently obvious the girl had a crush on him.

His use of the power of his potent masculinity to get his way made her lip curl a little. Martin had done that, dazzling her with his sexual charisma until it had ceased to be of any use to him. A cynical little smile curved her lips, followed by a shamed flush when she realised that Alick was watching her, heavy lids lowered. Flinching, she lifted her chin a little to parry the cold speculation in his eyes with defiance and a hint of scorn.

'Now,' Sophie interrupted, apparently noticing nothing, 'do your—does your mother know where you are?'

Aura's radiant face sobered. 'No,' she admitted. 'At least, I did tell them I was coming up here, but I don't think they believed me.'

'So you're going to ring them now and tell them, aren't you?' Alick prompted, his tone light and teasing, but that implacable note underlining the fact that the suggestion was, in fact, an order.

Aura sent him a wary, fleeting glance but bargained stoutly, 'If I can stay here for Christmas.'

'Darling,' Sophie said, her gaze flying to Alick's face, 'we'd like nothing better, you know that, but your mother will miss you. Christmas is a special time for families.'

Aura's lovely face was marred by a smile that no sixteen-year-old should ever wear. 'Not mine,' she said with a jauntiness that didn't hide the dreadful hurt beneath. 'They are going to the Browns' big bash, to which *I'm* not invited. Mum said I had to stay with the Petersons, whom I do not like. Derek keeps trying to back me into corners to kiss me, and he has wet lips and won't take no for an answer.'

Again, Sophie and Alick exchanged a look. Whether Aura had used this reason deliberately or not, there was no mistaking the revulsion and hidden fear in her expression.

'All right,' Alick said after a stretched moment. 'Put a call through to your mother and I'll talk to her.'

Aura bounced up from her chair and hugged Sophie and then him with an enthusiasm that said much about the precarious state of her confidence. Clearly, she hadn't been in the least sure that she would be allowed to stay.

As she went with Alick out of the room, Sophie sighed. 'Some people should never have children,' she said sadly.

Mrs Webster nodded in sympathy. 'I gather she doesn't like her stepfather?'

'I'm afraid not. She's certainly a handful, but he's never made any attempt to get on with her. He always felt that her mother was too easy on her. Mind you, he has a point. Her mother is one of those silly women who relies completely on the man in her life. It drove Aura's father away, although nothing to my mind can excuse a man who discards his child like a piece of old clothing. Aura adored him, and I think half her problem is that she feels that in some way it was her fault he deserted them. Unfortunately Lional Halswell is a martinet, so of course Aura has fought him all the way. Before her mother married him Aura had spent two years living in the sole charge of a woman whose idea of discipline was to sigh, "Dear, Mummy doesn't like that!" You can imagine just how effective *that* was with a high-spirited, energetic little thing like Aura.' She snorted. 'And you can imagine the battles they had with her after her mother married again. Fortunately, the child has always adored Alick, and I must say that he's been very good to her—and very good for her! As you saw.'

'Will she keep that promise not to hitch-hike?' Laurel asked curiously.

Sophie looked a little taken aback. 'Oh, yes, she's absolutely reliable. That's part of the trouble—she says what she thinks, and doesn't know the meaning of tact! But she'll do what Alick wants even though it takes a tussle of wills to persuade her. She has such a loving heart and she tries so hard to hide it. Poor child, I worry about her. Well, we all do. If only she weren't so pretty!'

On which remark she bustled out to see to preparing a room for the new arrival, leaving Laurel and her mother looking thoughtfully at each other.

Half an hour later, Alick had left, after extracting permission from Aura's mother for her to spend Christmas and New Year with the Forsythes. Fizzing with delight and excess energy, Aura was urging a reluctant

Laurel to put on her swimming 'togs' and go with her to Alick's pool to cool off.

Recognising that the excuses that had sufficed to placate Sophie were not going to work here, Laurel gave in with a set smile and went off up to her room to change, hoping that Alick was working somewhere on the orchard, anywhere but near his house.

After donning the sleek green maillot for the first time since she had bought it, she pulled on a sundress and slid her feet into sandals, then collected a swimming towel from the cupboard Sophie had shown her and with an odd resignation went down the stairs.

Aura was waiting, her lovely body encased in fashionable baggy shorts and a big loose shirt, chatting animatedly to Sophie and Maureen, all the dramatic sulkiness wiped from her face.

'Gosh, you look good,' she said cheerfully, beaming at Laurel. 'Cool and self-contained—very chic. Although you should have a big string of African beads around your neck to set that sundress off.'

'Aura,' Sophie said drily.

But the younger girl just grinned and shook her curls at her. 'I'll never be tactful,' she said cheerfully. 'And when it comes to clothes I'm usually right. Come on, Laurel, I'm dying of heat exhaustion.'

Certainly it was hot; the sun poured down remorselessly as they made their way through the stillness of the orchard. As they walked through the thick silence, not speaking, the only noise was the sibilant buzzings of insects they disturbed. Heat seemed to press them into the ground, making each footstep an effort, prickling against skin that was smothered in cream. Laurel knew that the smooth ivory of her skin was flushed with an apricot stain. She gave a grimace of distaste as she pushed her fingers through the wet locks of hair sticking to her temples and at the nape of her neck.

'For a while there I thought Alick might send me back,' Aura murmured as they came up to the complex.

'Lord, but he was furious when I told him I'd hitched up.'

'I can imagine.'

Aura sent her a keen glance. 'Aren't you going to tell me that it was a stupid thing to do?'

'I imagine,' Laurel said easily, 'that you already know that.'

Aura chuckled. 'If I hadn't, Alick made sure I soon did. He went all quiet and clipped; he never shouts when he's mad, but oh, man, can he tear strips off you! I hate it when he's furious with me, he makes me feel small and wormy. Still, he doesn't hold grudges. An almighty telling-off and that's it, sweetness and light until the next time I do something stupid. Are you his latest girlfriend?'

'No.'

'Hmm.' Aura surveyed her rigid, controlled profile. 'I was thrilled when Mum let out that he'd dumped Jenna. I don't know why he took up with her in the first place. She's so young!'

In spite of her discomfort Laurel couldn't stop the smile that lightened the amber depths of her eyes.

'I'm a hell of a lot older than her in most ways,' Aura said, reading her mind with uncanny ease. 'And I was surprised because Alick's too clever to need open adoration. I mean, she never contradicted him, you could tell when she looked at him that she thought he was absolutely perfect. He must have been bored out of his skull.'

'Some men like uncritical adoration,' Laurel said with a dry emphasis that made Aura frown.

'Alick doesn't,' she said after a thoughtful moment. 'He's too strong. I know the sort of man who needs a clinging dependent woman. My stepfather's one. He has to have someone to hang on his every word, do what he says, make him the centre of her universe, because that's the only way he can feel like a big, strong masculine man instead of the creep he really is. Independent people threaten him, make him feel small. Alick's not like that. He's tough. And he's honest.'

Out of the mouths of babes and sucklings! Laurel eyed her with dawning respect. She had just described Martin, who had needed to feel that he was the centre of his own universe. Perhaps he too had been gnawed by a sense of his inferiority.

It was a new concept, and one she pondered as they walked around the side of Alick's house to the pool, gleaming blue in the green expanse of the lawn. At one end was a paved extension of the terrace with another pergola overhead, sheltering a small pool-house and several chairs and a table from the sun. Laurel looked over her shoulder at the house.

'He's in Kerikeri,' Aura said smugly. 'He's got an appointment with someone and he won't be back until late.'

So you can relax, her tone implied.

Laurel bit her lip, aware that that look had given her away. Aura was altogether too astute, and although she was clearly suffering a massive crush on the man she called her cousin she seemed disposed to be friendly to someone she had apparently diagnosed as being in a similar state.

She was probably right, Laurel decided acidly. After all, whatever it was that she felt for Alick was hardly love.

'You can use the pool-house if you want to,' Aura said with an offhand wave at the building, 'but I'm just going to put my clothes on the back of a chair, seeing as no one's here.'

It seemed a reasonable idea. Wriggling free from the sundress, Laurel put it tidily over the back of a chair, then turned towards Aura. Her eyes widened. Compared to the younger woman's bathing-suit her own was more than conventional; it was dowdy. Aura wore an extreme version with the high-cut leglines that Laurel felt uncomfortable in, and a neckline that plunged almost to her navel, yet for all the overt sexuality of the scanty black thing it suited Aura's slenderness perfectly.

Laurel's brows rose. 'I'll bet your stepfather didn't approve of that,' she observed with a wry smile.

The one that answered it was sheer wickedness. 'He hasn't seen it yet,' Aura said, adding happily, 'but when he does he's going to really blow his stack. He already thinks I dress like a tart, so when I saw this I thought, right, I'll show him what a tart really dresses like!'

Laurel felt a pang of sympathy for her. 'It looks stunning,' she said lightly, 'as I'm sure you know, but don't be surprised if the first man to see you in it has a stroke.'

To her surprise Aura blushed, before saying carelessly, 'Oh, it will only be Alick, and he doesn't think of me as anything but his little cousin.'

Watching her dive neatly into the water Laurel wondered rather bleakly if that was true. Perhaps Alick— no, that didn't add up at all. Aura was truly beautiful, but she was only sixteen, and Alick had certainly looked at her with the affection and exasperation of an older brother rather than the appreciation of a man who saw a woman he wanted.

As he had looked at her, she thought dreamily, with that steel-blue gleam of passion in his eyes and his countenance sharpened by desire.

'Come on, Laurel, the water's like silk!'

Her reverie interrupted, she too dived in, gasping at first at the contrast of water and air, then revelling in the cool freedom of the water, the weightless buoyancy. She struck up for the surface and began to swim, enjoying the stretching of muscles as she propelled herself with smooth, even strokes through the water, length after length after length.

'Hey, you can swim,' Aura said, eyeing her with respect when at last she swam up to the side of the pool.

'I love it.' Laurel pushed the hair back from her eyes, her glowing face revealing the truth of her words.

'Have you got a pool?'

She nodded. 'A tiny one compared to this.'

'Oh, I suppose Alick needs a big one, he's so big himself, isn't he? And he likes swimming, too.' Her brilliant eyes focused on a point just behind Laurel; she grinned as she said, 'Hello, Alick. You should see Laurel swim! She did sixty lengths of the pool!'

'You counted?'

How could a voice so deep and rough feel like velvet stroking along her nerves?

Aura grinned, the little minx, keeping her gaze very carefully fixed on Alick, but Laurel could see that she was up to something.

'Yes, I counted. Are you coming in with us?'

'I think I might.'

From the corner of her eye Laurel watched him walk over to the pool-house; her whole instinct was to leap out of the pool and flee back to the comparative safety of the homestead, but with Aura sitting there it would look too pointed. Calmly she decided that she would stay in for a short time and then tell them that she was tired and that she wanted to go back. They couldn't complain about that. After all, Aura had given her the perfect excuse; all those lengths had tired her out.

She was lying on her back in the water when she saw him on the side of the pool, standing with his hands on his hips, watching her with the hooded predatory stare of a hunter. Her heart turned over in her breast as a hot flood of sensation flowed from her limbs to the pit of her stomach, setting fire to each cell as it passed.

The sun gilded his skin, transforming him into a golden man, magnificent as an idol worshipped in some old scandalous religion. Like Aura he wore black, sleek racers, and like hers his hid nothing, skimming his narrow hips and moulding themselves to the firm flatness of his stomach and the tight muscles of his backside.

The promise of potency that was the first thing Laurel had noticed about him, the explicit sexuality of a virile male animal, was tempered by cool arrogance, the hard confidence of a man who was master of himself and his life. And with it all was an elemental danger, a dark summons to all that was female in her, promising the fulfilment of all her forbidden desires.

He gave her a sardonic smile. With her breath locked somewhere in her throat she watched the muscles ripple and flow as he cut into the water in a shallow racing dive.

CHAPTER SEVEN

AURA'S voice intruded into the sensuous enchantment. Looking profoundly pleased with herself she said, in a tone so casual that Laurel's eyes flew suspiciously to her complacent face, 'I think I'll head back now, Laurel, I'm starting to burn. Say goodbye to Alick for me, will you?'

'Hey, wait a minute...'

But the wretched girl hauled herself out of the pool and, moving with a speed that was astonishing, wrapped that delectable body in a towel, slid her feet into rubber sandals, and shot across the lawn.

Laurel started and looked around as a subdued swirl of water announced Alick's reappearance. Grinning, he watched Aura's departing figure with amusement.

'No one,' he drawled, 'could accuse her of being subtle, could they? I've no doubt she thinks she's being terribly tactful.'

And suddenly the funny side of the situation quirked Laurel's mouth up in an answering grin. 'She's a monster,' she said.

'Amiable, however, and with very definite ideas on almost everything. She has decided that you must be here for one reason only, and as her continued sojourn here depends on keeping me sweet, then keep me sweet she definitely will. Even if it means throwing you to the wolves. Or wolf. She's still young enough to get a secret thrill from the idea of a rake.'

Colour scalded through Laurel's skin. She hated the mockery in the dark depths of his eyes, hated the smooth blandness of his tones.

'Did you tell her that——?' She hesitated, the tide of colour deepening as his brows lifted. However he said nothing, and she had to continue, 'Did you give her any indication that—that——?'

'That we were having an affair?' he supplied helpfully.

'We are not having an affair!' The words tumbled from her outraged mouth.

He grinned and extended a wet forefinger to the pulse that throbbed in the hollow of her throat. A stab of excitement speared through her and the amusement in his eyes was burned away by a darker, more intense emotion.

'No, I didn't tell her anything,' he said, watching as his hand spread out, warm and cool at the same time, powerful in its casual strength across the warm ivory breadth of her shoulder.

Like her he seemed fascinated by the difference in their skin tones, the golden tan of his lean fingers barbarically blatant against the smooth, wet slickness of her shoulder. When she shivered his eyes flew upwards, impaling her with such naked hunger that she gasped.

'No,' he repeated, a grim little smile curling the cruel beauty of his mouth, 'I'm not in the habit of confiding in sixteen-year-olds, but Aura doesn't need telling. She's become very astute over the years at picking up signals; in a way it's been a matter of survival for her. She knew that I wanted you the night of the party at my house.'

His thumb was moving across her throat, soft and gentle, brushing slowly. The tiny unseen hairs on Laurel's skin rose, dragging it tight with unbearable anticipation.

She swallowed. 'But you weren't . . .' she whispered, the words heavy on her tongue.

'Don't be so obtuse. The first time I looked at you, my whole body clenched with need. Why do you think I was so obnoxious? I don't normally treat perfectly pleasant young women who end up on my doorstep with such patent rudeness. I saw you staring at me with that stunned absorption and I wanted to take you inside and make myself master of everything, your pretty face, your lithe body, become so much a part of you that when you ate you tasted me, when you slept I was all that you dreamed of.'

Unbearably stimulated by his words, she shivered.

His mouth twisted. 'But I'd been that way before.'

Michelle, she thought feverishly, remembering the gossip that Blair had passed on at the diamond wedding celebrations. He had had an affair with a married woman called Michelle, an affair that had gone sour. Was he intimating that this need that savaged her was in the same order as that other scandalous affair? Had Michelle looked like her, small and voluptuous, a 'pocket Venus'? An icy chill shafted through the heat of his caress.

Was this how Alick had felt when she had told him that she only wanted him because he looked like Martin? Humiliation and anger combining into a black fury?

His mouth hardened into a straight line. 'And I was engaged to Jenna. I had no intention of breaking the engagement. Then.'

Her jealous pain was quenched by the soft touch of his finger on her mouth. A small drum beat feverishly in her heart, keeping time with the rising flame of anticipation searing through her. She touched her tongue to her dry lips and found his finger, hard and slightly salty. Her tongue curled around it, then withdrew, panicked by his expression, the sudden tormented need that darkened his eyes as they followed the little movement. Tiny flecks of gold in the dark blue irises were swallowed up with mesmerising speed by the expanding pupils until his gaze was black with desire.

Laurel made a desperate grab for sanity, closing her eyes against the hypnotism of his intense stare. 'I don't— I can't . . .' she said frantically.

He laughed softly and the sensations assailing her coalesced into exquisite pain, transformed into an intolerable craving. With a stifled murmur she swayed towards him, the logical instructions of her brain banished by this overwhelming sensuality.

The kiss was everything she had dreamed of, gentle at first, reassuring her into acceptance, and then not gentle at all, forcing her head back across his arm as he took passionate possession of her mouth. Willingly she accepted the hard thrust of his tongue.

Alick laughed deep in his throat, the husky satisfied laugh of a man who knew that he had mastered his woman, and took all that she offered him, searching out every sweet recess, expunging with his kiss all memories of other kisses, another man.

Slowly she became aware of other things, of the heat of his body against hers, the strength of the arm that held her crushed against him, the burgeoning of his loins in their sleek black covering beneath the water.

They might just as well have been naked for the two thin layers of fabric between them hid nothing. So lost was Laurel in a sensual haze that she forgot every hard-learned lesson, every cruel fact. She knew only that this man was infinitely desirable to her, that the racing, thudding skip-beats of her heart were the counterpoint to a tide of uncontrollable passion surging through every cell and nerve-end in her body.

She arched into him, desperate to ease her hunger in the driving force of his manhood, and he lifted his head and said in a rough voice, 'Not here, Laurel.'

She thought she heard contempt in the gravelly tones. Shuddering, she suddenly realised what she was inviting. An icy wash of shamed panic wrenched her free of his embrace. For a moment she stood quiescent, her breath tearing through her lungs, watching with unseeing eyes the sharp rise and fall of his broad chest. Her skin prickled, and she caught her trembling lip with savage force between her teeth, striving valiantly for some sort of control, something to curb this runaway need.

Oh, God, she wanted him so much! She wanted to take him into her, she wanted to feel his weight, the strength and power of his body, lose herself in the age-old movements of love. Balked of the culmination of ecstasy, her body mourned, the heady fumes of desire fogging her brain so that she couldn't think, couldn't speak.

With a trembling hand she pushed a strand of hair back from her cheek, her eyes sliding sideways to fix on to the tiles bordering the pool.

He said quietly, 'You're shivering. Come on, let's get out.'

She was grateful that he didn't touch her. It took an effort of will to get up on to the edge of the pool, and once she was there she had to hug herself to stop the betraying shudders that were racking her body. After a long moment they eased enough to pass for shivers, but her heart was still thudding high in her throat and unsatisfied passion gnawed through her.

Winding the towel around herself in a vain effort to hide from him, she said woodenly, 'I'd better get back.'

He tipped her chin, and when she flinched he frowned. 'Look at me,' he commanded.

Her lashes fluttered but she didn't raise them. He said, 'Laurel, what's the matter?'

This time she did look at him, and his face stiffened. 'What is it?' he demanded.

'Nothing.'

His eyes bored into hers and in their depths she saw a fire begin to glow. 'Have you been abused?' he asked.

His voice was so quiet that she should have relaxed, but what she saw in his eyes and read in his face made her blood congeal in her heart.

'No,' she whispered.

'Then why are you so afraid?'

She knew now why Aura had given in. The steady flame of anger allied to the hard determination of his expression in his eyes was truly intimidating. She bit her lip, afraid to tell him that she was flawed, that she couldn't bear to give herself to him only to see his desire fade when confronted by her inability to respond.

She knew that he would not be cruel as Martin had been; there was no petulance or viciousness in his make-up. No, she didn't fear that. What she couldn't cope with was the anguish that would claim her when his passion was replaced by indifference, the inevitable arrival of the day when he would look at her and see, not a woman he wanted to make love to, but one who was not a true woman, a sexless neuter who could neither give nor receive satisfaction.

Satisfaction! How she hated that word, yet once she would have been content to achieve it. Now, she was horrified to realise that she wanted much more than the mere gratification of a physical itch. She wanted fulfilment, rapture, ecstasy, and in this man's arms. What kind of bitter fate had doomed her to being only half a woman?

Shamed misery darkened her eyes to a muddy brown, all the colour and life erased from them. She thought he didn't believe her denial of abuse, but his relentless gaze softened as it dwelt on her trembling mouth.

'It's all right,' he said beneath his breath, and released her chin. She tried to step away but the breath hurt in her lungs when he eased her into a curiously comforting, asexual embrace. 'Don't worry, sweetheart; whatever it is, we'll deal with it together. And I promise I won't push. You're a very wary little bird and I've already rushed things. We'll take things easily from now on.'

She had to tell him *now*. Pulling away, she said in a voice that sounded stilted and strained, 'There's nothing to work through. I don't want you to deal with anything. I don't want you, Alick.'

Those unsparing eyes scanned the shadowed contours of her face from the peachy softness of her mouth to the broad vulnerable temples, measuring, assessing, searching through the thin camouflage of her pride to the truth below.

'You're lying,' he said uncompromisingly. 'Why, Laurel? That wasn't a lack of response I felt a few minutes ago when we were kissing in the pool.'

She bit her lip, then said with harsh distinctness, 'I don't want an affair with you, Alick, and that's all it would be.'

Something flickered deep in his eyes, and although she couldn't see any change in his expression she knew that he had come to a decision.

'I see,' he said softly, and grinned, a reckless, swashbuckling smile that reminded her irresistibly of his Viking ancestors: ruthless and brutal, yet possessors of such a profound aesthetic sense that their longships and other artefacts still appealed to connoisseurs of beauty.

'Then I'll just have to change your mind,' he told her calmly.

Pain jagged through; pain mixed with anger. 'Don't you understand? I *don't want* an affair with you. I realise that probably no one has ever turned you down before, but I'm doing it now.'

'I've been turned down,' he said indifferently, lifting a taunting eyebrow at her open incredulity. His mouth eased from a hard slash to mockery, but beneath that was a purposefulness she found chilling. 'However, I'm going to take it as a good sign that you find it hard to believe. If you can give me one reason why you don't want us to become lovers, perhaps I'll listen.'

She almost told him then but pride stopped the bitter words; she couldn't bear to watch his expression change to disgust. Far better for him to assume that she just didn't want to get caught up in an affair.

'No?' He grinned, making no attempt to hide his bone-deep confidence, the frightening self-assurance of a man who had no intention of giving up. 'Then I'll make a deal with you. We take things slowly. No more madness in swimming-pools, just a quiet time getting to know each other over Christmas and New Year. And then you can decide whether you want to take it further. All right?'

He was up to something, he had to be. Suspiciously, she asked, 'And what do you get out of that?'

The amusement vanished to be replaced by cool scorn. 'The pleasure of your company,' he said in a level voice.

Fretfully she rubbed at her forehead, aware that she yearned to agree, to share some part of his life with him in spite of the fact that it would be so much harder to leave him in the end.

'Contrary to what you so obviously think,' he bit out, watching her with that unnerving intentness, 'I can enjoy the less physical aspects of—getting to know a woman.'

Still she hesitated, her indecision plain, and he laughed without humour and said casually, 'I'll take your agreement for granted. Come on, we'd better start making tracks or Sophie will begin composing wedding invitations.'

She flushed again, embarrassed by Sophie's match-making. 'Clearly,' she said shortly as she walked across the lawn with him, 'she's eager to get you married.'

'Sophie's positive that marriage is the only thing that will tame me,' he returned, still in that detached voice. 'She feels it's time I settled down. If you like, I'll have a word with her so that she doesn't embarrass you any more.'

She sighed, unwillingly seeing the funny side of it. 'You'd better have a word with Aura, too,' she said ruefully.

He slanted her a mocking look, the hard lines of his mouth twisted. 'It would be easier if we——'

'No!'

'All right,' he said, apparently not at all upset by the explosive force of the monosyllable. 'Come on, I'll drive you back.'

She said steadily. 'I'd rather walk back, if you don't mind. By myself.'

He surprised her by agreeing without any further demur, and she was irritated by the fact that his acqui-escence annoyed her.

But, on her trip back across the silent, heat-humming orchard blocks, she made a few decisions. For some reason he had given her a breathing-space. She was almost certain that he had no intention of letting her decide against an affair; he would definitely try to change her mind! Alick was not the sort of man who meekly yielded to setbacks, so why should he be any different when it came to his love life?

But she would play along with him, keeping him at a distance while she was in Kerikeri, and then she would run back to Auckland. Once there it would be much easier to keep out of his way, and sooner or later he would realise that she had meant it when she said she didn't want an affair with him.

And she would have the memory of this summer holiday to keep her happy during the long cold years when she was once more alone.

The decision made, she had only to summon up the will-power to stick to it.

In the subsequent days he was never very far from her, and during the festivities that wound down the year he made his interest patently clear, sending off one or two interested men with an icy-eyed dispatch that shocked her even as it gave rise to an age-old thrill. She stopped looking for Jenna after discovering that she and her family were spending the holiday season with a sister in the South Island, and slowly, as golden day followed golden day, Laurel let her guilt sink beneath a tide of happiness.

True to Alick's word there was no more kissing, but he was not constrained by his promise. He took every opportunity to be close to her, dancing with her whenever possible, holding her against him when they went out sailing together in a sleek fifteen-foot catamaran, so that she could feel his laughter and exhilaration as the craft's two hulls sliced through the green water of the Kerikeri inlet on a day that had been made in paradise.

Oh, he knew how to wind a woman around those lean strong fingers. He had lied, too; or at the very least misdirected her. Breathing-space, indeed! He used the time to woo her with laughter and argument, the potent alchemy of fleeting caresses, the deep pleasure of pitting her wits against his, of making discoveries about him, satisfying her curiosity, appeasing some primal yearning to know all about him, understand him...

And every hour of every day, through the parties and the picnics, through the contentment of Christmas Day to the unalloyed fun of New Year, always there was the slow burn of sensuality just beneath the surface, the sizzling magic of glances that met and locked, the potency of desire made stronger for its ruthless imprisonment.

As she packed her bags the day before they were to go back to Auckland, Laurel thought that she seemed to have been living in a glass bowl, able to see out but separated from the others by an impermeable barrier. She knew that everyone, even Aura, hoped that they were watching a love-story, little realising that this one had no happy ending.

Oh, occasionally, when she was even more on edge, kept awake by the urgings of a body denied fulfilment, she asked herself why she didn't just surrender, make love and see what happened.

She wanted him so much; perhaps with him she would be able to respond. Perhaps he would burn away her inhibitions in the fire of his sexuality.

But cold, crisp common sense told her she was yearning after the impossible. After all, she had wanted Martin. It had been nothing like this incandescent ache for completeness, but she had wanted him and she had gone happily to her wedding night.

The defect was in her because there had been other women for Martin, women he had thrilled with his passion. When he had realised that she could not respond, he had flung his success with others in her face, hurling their names like ugly pebbles, reducing her to beaten silence because she could not satisfy him. Somewhere, she had missed out on an important part of every woman's heritage, and she was less than other women because of it.

No, things were better as they were. She couldn't bear to think of disillusion in Alick's harshly sculptured face, the bleak light of knowledge in his dark eyes. Better by far that he think she had lost interest, that she didn't love him.

There, she had said it; admitted the knowledge that had been knocking on the edge of her consciousness for weeks.

She loved Alick Forsythe.

And because she loved him she would have to leave him, turn her back on him and walk away into the sterile life she had chosen. These last lovely days had taught her that he was an intensely sensual man. He touched her with the same tactile sensitivity that was apparent when he touched a flower, or a shell he had picked up from the sand. He looked at her with the same delight that he looked at the Bay of Islands spread out below them; he used all of his senses with frank enjoyment, as she knew he would use them in making love. He deserved a woman who could respond to his passion with an equal commitment, not one who was so seriously flawed that she lay stiff with embarrassment and revulsion in his arms, striving to hide her lack of response, and failing miserably.

Even now, safe in her bedroom, the bad memories had the power to make her cringe. It would, she thought miserably, be like a kind of death, and she could not do it. She loved him too much to do it to him, and she was too proud to have him know her secret. Better to let his desire for her die naturally, as it would when she was in Auckland and he was up here, than to have him remember her as frigid. At least that way she might salvage something; he might remember her with affection.

He gave them all dinner at his place that night, a delicious meal cooked by the woman who did his housework and cooked several meals each week for him. It was a delightful evening, laughter mingling with a gentle longing because it was their last night, and when the others went home he said quietly, 'Stay with me and help me clean up.'

She nodded, knowing that it was dangerous, knowing that if she had any sense she would go back with the others who were smiling significantly at them now; but her hungry heart wanted something more to mark the end of her idyll, this happiest time in her life, and so she stayed, waving the big Daimler off, her hand clasped in his.

They put the dishes into the dishwasher and cleaned up the immaculate kitchen, talking like old friends while the undercurrent of tension ran like quicksilver between them.

She wondered if he would ask for her decision, but, although his eyes lingered on her mouth and the long creamy line of her throat and the soft contours of her breasts beneath the peach dress, he said nothing. Laurel didn't know whether to be happy or sad.

She did know that every time their eyes met, every time she heard his voice or caught sight of his strong profile, her insides melted.

And that working beside him like this was painfully sweet, mocking the hidden thoughts she had not even dared to admit to, the fantasies of being his wife.

'Come on out on to the terrace and we'll have a nightcap,' he said, smiling at her with something very like irony in his eyes.

She nodded, her heart thudding rapidly in her breast.

He followed her out on to the deck, moving with the lethal grace that so intimidated her. Sadness and the strain of savagely restraining her hunger for so long had worn down her wariness. She just felt tired.

Lifting her face to the sky, she was aware of him moving silently behind her, but even so it was a shock when he bent and kissed her, a shock that held her passive beneath the warm pressure of his mouth. After a moment he lifted his head and looked down at her, his face sharply carved in the bold barbaric lines of a warrior.

'Still fighting?'

Her heart began to race. 'What do you mean?'

Something smouldered in the depths of his narrowed eyes. 'You think you've managed to control what you feel for me, don't you? I felt it when I kissed you. The iron bars of restraint clanged down. You think you've managed to kill that incandescent response.'

'I have,' she said bluntly, her heart writhing in pain as she lied.

His smile was twisted, and she caught her breath. He had never looked so dangerous as he did now.

'No,' he said softly, holding her gaze with the heated lambent flame of his. 'You're running, Laurel, running so scared that you don't understand what you're doing.'

'I am not afraid!'

'Yes, you are. You've been terrified ever since the first time you saw me.'

She tried to deflect him with an indignant, 'I'm not used to having half-naked men open the door to me!'

'It wasn't just that, and you know it. You looked at me with a kind of dazed lust, and I felt myself respond, mindlessly, with a hidden compulsion that frightened me too.'

'Jenna——'

'—is irrelevant. As irrelevant as that twisted idiot you were stupid enough to marry because you thought his need to own you body and soul was love. Your bad experience with him is the reason you won't give us a chance, isn't it?'

Colour drained from her skin, leaving her white and cold with apprehension. In a voice that shook, she said, 'You've been talking to——'

'Your mother? Yes, I had to, as it was obvious you weren't going to tell me anything about your marriage. And that's where the problem is, isn't it, rooted in your marriage? You lied, Laurel. You told me he didn't abuse you.'

'He didn't,' she whispered, horror numbing her brain. 'Mum wouldn't have told you he hit me!'

He shook her gently. 'Abuse doesn't have to be physical. Maureen said——'

'How dare you discuss me with my mother?' A frantic terror fuelled her rage; even as she gasped the words out she realised that of course her mother wouldn't have told him her daughter was hopeless as a lover.

He smiled, a savage set movement of his hard mouth, and caught her up to him, controlling her wriggling, struggling form with effortless ease as he stepped down into the sitting-out place by the little waterfall.

'I dare quite easily,' he said, mocking her as he sat down on the wide green cushions, still holding her imprisoned in his strong arms. 'I have waited long enough for you, Laurel, and now it's time to collect.'

He silenced her futile protests in the easiest, most basic way of all: with his mouth.

It took her by surprise so that her lips opened beneath his in a little gasp, and before she had time to realise it the fortress walls had fallen, and she was submerged beneath a wave of passion so overpowering that she could only grasp his shoulders and give him what he demanded—her complete surrender.

She had nothing to fight him with. Completely at his mercy, her hidden desires were laid bare, her needs brutally exposed. Against her lips his mouth was fierce and demanding, crushing their softness in a kiss that should have terrified the life out of her.

But passion overrode fear in a swirl of drama, scarlet shot through with black. With the cool music of the tiny waterfall tinkling peacefully a few feet away, Laurel learned the depths and strength of her need, the aching hunger that lay in wait for her, the willing treachery of every cell in her body.

Immediately he felt her response his mouth gentled, softened, and she relaxed, thinking dazedly that it was over, he had proved his point. But the moment he sensed the death of her resistance his tongue flicked along the crushed silk of her lips in a caress as erotic as it was unexpected. Her mouth dried and her lips parted anew in surprise. With a muffled laugh he deepened the caress into another kiss, delving into the sweet recesses with an intent purposefulness that had her heart thundering in her chest. The tumultuous leap of desire in her blood made her groan beneath that thrusting kiss.

'Yes,' he said.

Her hands were clutching the front of his shirt; with his mouth still on hers he reached down and unfolded them, guiding her fingers beneath the fine cotton to his chest.

He was so hot! Like heated satin, his skin was smooth and tight over tense muscles, and then roughened by the fine overlay of hair. She remembered that sensation, silk and satin, and the heat rising beneath her tentative fingertips. But Martin had objected to her touching him; he had said she was clumsy, she didn't know what to do to pleasure a man.

The thought of the man who had been her husband made her stiffen and try to jerk her hand away, until Alick muttered, 'Don't panic, I'm not going to hurt you, I promise.'

Soothed by the stark honesty in his voice, she relaxed, her small stiff body easing to fit the strong lines of his, her hand insensibly beginning to stroke across the wide chest.

'Oh, God, yes,' he encouraged, his mouth sliding from the sensitive spot beneath her ear to the even more sensitive area where her neck joined her shoulder. 'Touch me, Laurel. I've wanted to know how your hands would feel on me for so long...'

He bit into the sleek ivory skin, gently and then not quite so gently, sending erotic little chills down her spine. Emboldened, she turned her head to return the caress, her small sharp teeth finding the smooth powerful swell of a muscle then smoothing over the tiny mark she made with her lips and her tongue.

Deep inside her something rejoiced at the shudder that shook his strong frame. With a soft murmur she pulled the buttons of his shirt open and allowed herself the luxury of pressing her face against his chest. He smelt so wonderful, slightly salty with more than a hint of musk, spicy and immensely appealing.

Aroused male.

He moved, and she froze, half expecting rejection, but he did no more than lean back against the side of the sitting-out place with his arms outstretched along the edge of the terrace floor so that he was completely exposed to her. She looked at him, tentative and wary.

'Take what you want,' he said softly.

For a heart-stopping second she hesitated, then sighed in surrender and leaned forward to kiss the strong column of his throat, her lips lingering against the cord that tensed there.

His expression absorbed yet almost withdrawn, he suffered her experimental, exploring hands with no signs of reaction but for the glitter in the deep eyes and the dappling of moisture across his skin. He was, she realised with an astonishment close to incredulity, letting her set the pace, not snatching his own pleasure and leaving her to garner what she could along the way.

Once more she looked up into the chiselled angles of his face, her intent, questioning gaze wandering from the tell-tale flush along the stark cheekbones to the sculpted lines of his mouth, that full bottom lip lending a disturbing sensuality to his expression.

She pushed the fine cotton of his shirt back, her hands visibly trembling but her mouth set in a way that denoted her determination. If this was all that she was going to have of him, she was going to do what she had dreamed of ever since she saw him; she was going to shape him with her hands and her mouth, touch him with the love that she dared not express, imprint him on her body memory, so that when she was old she would only need to close her eyes and she would experience him as he was now, sleek and powerful, the fine dusting of body hair making antique scrolls across the width of his chest, the splendid shoulders rippling with muscle beneath skin like oiled silk.

Absorbed, her eyes half closed, she traced out the smooth, powerful muscles, kissing along the taut contours, holding back the fiery impulse that made her long to close her teeth together in a bite that stung, mark him with her teeth and her nails in a primitive rite of ownership, then soothe the pain away with the soft magic of her lips.

His eyes were almost hidden by the heavy lids, but she saw fire gleaming behind them, and a deep hunger that ate into her bones, setting fire to them, a flame that joined the conflagration in the juncture of her thighs.

A mirthless smile creased his lean cheek. He bent his head and kissed her with the slow, experienced seduction of expertise, his hot, fierce mouth made all the more potent by the ferocious control he was exercising. All resistance fled; with a soft little groan she gave him what he demanded, her body throbbing with the need to press herself against him, her loins throbbing with frustration.

He too was affected by the stark sensuality of their embrace. Beneath her she could feel the tautness of his heavily muscled thighs, the stirring masculine power. Always before it had repelled her, but this time some primitive part of her revelled in the knowledge that she was able to do this to him.

'Yes,' he said thickly, his mouth only a whisper away from the vulnerable hollow in her throat. 'It's hard for a man to hide that he's aroused. How about you, Laurel?

Does your body know yet that it has met its other half? Let's see, shall we?'

His hand skimmed the tip of her breast. She gasped as the tender aureoles stiffened, lifting proudly, pleading for more. Dumbly, she watched while his eyes lingered on the soft mounds of her breasts beneath that questing, almost insulting touch.

'So far so good,' he murmured. 'Do they hurt, Laurel, sweet wanton, little temptress? Do they ache for my mouth as much as I ache for the tight, hot grip of your satin body?'

A convulsive shudder shook her as she turned her flushed face away, unable to meet his unsparing survey. Calmly, skilfully, he pushed the top of her dress down over her shoulders, the collar and sleeves forming a kind of vice around her upper arms so that she was unable to free herself. But one hand could reach the dark honey of his hair as he lowered his head, and when at last his mouth found the point of fire in her breast she clasped him against her and yielded herself up to the voluptuous, exquisite sensations with a shivering sigh that held nothing but surrender.

The little waterfall tinkled down, the porcelain dragon watched with his knowing, unnerving eyes, as Laurel gave up any pretence of resistance, following Alick wherever he took her. She forgot about her experience with Martin, she forgot that always before she had endured making love and ended up at the least unsatisfied and frustrated, mostly sickened and disgusted.

For Alick used the innate power of his virility to woo her and seduce her into first acquiescence and then eager incarceration in the prison of desire he was constructing about her. First of all he gentled her, so that she became accustomed to his hands on her skin, the strength of his lean body, the heated regard and the sheer magic of his mouth as it traced its wooing enchantment over her shaking, expectant body. She discovered aching anticipation at his hand on her breasts, tense eagerness when she waited for his kisses, the slow smooth slide of skin against skin, punctuated by the runaway thudding of hearts caught in this sensual mutual voyage of discovery.

But when his hand slid through the soft folds of her petticoat to her thigh she flinched and froze, knowing what to expect now, the quick greedy probing, the painful exploration and the sudden assault.

'Relax,' he said quietly. 'I won't do any more than you wish, I promise you.'

Her lips moved in a bleak ironic smile. She knew how much such promises were worth. Experience told her that once things got this far there was no turning back. And in a way she was glad; at least he would know that she wasn't able to respond. And when that was over he would leave her alone.

Beyond that she refused to look.

But he had behaved with a tender, purposeful restraint up until then, and her whole body was aching with a thousand unknown needs, so she lay along the wide cushions on the bench and waited for him to finish what he had started.

'Don't look so martyred,' he said harshly, judging her reactions with an accuracy that startled her. 'It's not going to hurt, Laurel. And, if you want me to, I can stop.'

As though to underline his statement his hand lay still against the sensitive skin of her thigh, so near to its goal, so frustratingly distant.

Scarlet, she avoided his eyes, her own fixed self-consciously on the white blossoms of the jasmine gleaming in the moonlight. The fact that he was able to think of stopping meant that she had not aroused him very much.

Martin had never been able to stop.

A sickening humiliation ate into her, setting fire to a sudden fierce anger. In spite of her fears she was still acutely sensitised to him, her skirt tight and stretched, her body melting with a feverish need. Even if making love arrived at its usual dismal conclusion for her, she needed to give Alick the surcease he wanted because she loved him, and her love transcended the physical attraction that had exploded like a flashfire to complicate her life.

'Can you?' she asked, not having to fake her languorous voice. Her hand slid through the tangle of hair on his chest, stroked downwards, and with a smile that trembled invitingly on her lips she unbuckled his belt, her eyes widening as his breath was sucked in harshly.

Her hand froze.

'Don't stop there,' he said harshly. 'Teasing without following through is likely to get you hurt, Laurel. Is that what you did to your husband?'

Her lips formed the negative but no sound came forth. Dragging some of the cool night air into her parched lungs she slid the zip of his trousers down, pulling the expensive cloth with it, her hands shaking at the enormity of what she was doing. He would think she was truly wanton, and no doubt he would despise her; but oh, she wanted him, she wanted to touch him as intimately as he was touching her, she wanted . . .

An elemental reaction immobilised his features into a stark mask save for the leaping wildness in his gaze. Eyes never leaving her face, his lean flexible hand moved, sliding quietly, slowly, patiently into her soft depths.

Sensation, pure and inconceivable, flooded her. The honeyed ache liquefied her loins. Caught by surprise, she cried out, her body bucking against the tormenting fingers.

'Relax,' he said again in that rough, impeded voice. 'Relax, yes, that's it, easy now . . .'

Raspy as it was, his voice soothed her, lulled her into accepting his touch. And he was so gentle, so skilful, that after a few seconds she relaxed, her astonished eyes held by the stark compulsion of his as the heat began to flicker again, beating up through her body, sweeping out of its path all fear and inhibitions in a dazzling flood of rapture.

He was magnificent, all taut muscle and sinew, skin gleaming in the adoring light of the stars like a pagan god of old, splendidly proportioned, radiant with power as he visited the maiden chosen for his nightly love-feast.

When she had touched him, accepted the intimate probe of his hand and the fire of his mouth, some reservation deep inside her, so far buried that she hadn't even known it existed, crumbled silently and inexorably into nothing, releasing for the first time in her life the full force of her feminine instincts.

Her body seemed to have a life of its own. She arched into the seeking strength of his hand, and a low, broken sound worked its way up from her throat. Her hands clenched across his back, pulling him into her as she nuzzled the heated expanse of his chest.

'Yes, you're ready,' he said, not even trying to hide the deep satisfaction in his voice.

She didn't care whether she was ready, she wanted nothing more than to be taken and possessed, her body a willing sacrifice on the altar of their desire, her torment eased in the only way possible at this moment.

She was smiling as he moved over her, her eyes open, her expression free from all shame and caution. Fearlessly, she looked up into his face, read the blazing desire there; fearlessly, every cell awash with a tide of passion, she welcomed the hard thrust, the smooth entrance, the final, jolting possession, the delicious weight of him.

It was for this moment that she had lived, this moment that she had been born for, when she lay in a flood of starshine, and with a stark primeval hunger gave herself to the man she loved.

But even as she felt the completion she had longed for she learned that there was more to come.

It was like the building of a storm, the jolting increments of danger and anticipation, until finally the lightning struck and thunder echoed around the hills while for a moment all creation held its breath. Laurel learned that danger had its own rewards, that surrender could lead to victory, that the world could narrow down to two people, a man and a woman, and that lightning could arc from one to the other, increasing with each shuddering thrust, each primeval response, until at last she was flung out beyond time and space into a place where the only reality was sensation, radiant as hope and as powerful as the eternal conflict of the elements.

With the echoes of her cry dying in her ears she felt Alick reach his peak, the fierce male body taut and exultant in its pride, and then after the exultation the subsidence into delicious lethargy.

Still shaking from her own glory, she welcomed his warm weight, her arms enfolding him, unable yet to tell him that she loved him, hoping that her embrace said it for her.

For of course she could say it now. The fear that had kept her imprisoned these last years had fled like darkness at the touch of the sun.

She lay silently, not thinking, letting the sound of the little waterfall tinkle through her brain, her half-closed eyes resting on the porcelain dragon. He was beautiful, she decided dreamily. Just beautiful, although it was not the conventional beauty. No; like Alick, his was the beauty of strength and power, of an age-old mystery. All male, potent with a power she barely understood even though it had touched her life and turned it inside out.

She was no longer threatened by his potent masculine sensuality. Later, she might mourn the loss of that excitement, the painful exhilaration, but at the moment relief flowed like wine through her veins, and the smile she gave was sleepily smug beneath the lingering wonder.

She felt as though she had faced the fire, walked through it unscathed and won triumph against terrible odds.

She smiled again, for there was nothing she could not do.

CHAPTER EIGHT

AT LAST Alick moved, ignoring Laurel's soft protest, and pulled on his clothes with lithe, swift movements.

She watched, openly adoring.

'You'll get cold,' he said, looking across. He kept oddly dispassionate eyes fixed firmly on to her face. 'Come on, put your clothes on.'

A small chill wound its way through her happiness, smearing its bright shiny fabric, and sure enough she shivered. Quickly, averting her eyes, she drew on her clothes, her fingers clumsy and cold as she fastened clips and buttons.

He stood watching her, the heavy lids hiding his thoughts, his expression so impassive that the cold chill of unease was a full-blown hurricane by the time she had finished.

Then he said calmly. 'Now, tell me that the only reason you want me is that I look like Martin bloody Du Fresne.'

Ice coagulated around her heart and encased her bones so that she thought that, if she moved, she might shatter into a million pieces. She couldn't breathe; her lungs felt as though she had been stabbed with knives.

'I——'

'Don't try lying,' he warned in that silky voice. 'You told me yourself that that was the sole reason you were attracted to me.'

She closed her eyes. Against the lids his image danced, lethal, a dark shadow against the darkness of her dreams. 'Yes,' she admitted in a low, shamed voice. 'I thought that was——'

'Why don't you say it? You wanted me because I look like your dead husband, the man who left you. Well, now you've had me. Was it worth it? How do I stack up against him? Tell me, Laurel.'

'It's not like that,' she whispered numbly, scarcely knowing what she was saying.

His voice cut contemptuously through her. 'It wasn't even as though he was decent to you. I've heard of women like you—abuse junkies, needing that fix, longing for men who are no good for them, unable to form any sort of relationship with a man unless he hurts them. That's sick, Laurel, self-destructive.'

She shrank back, sickened. 'I am not like that,' she said thinly.

'You need help.'

She flinched. 'No!'

Scorn iced his words. 'You're not going to improve until you've admitted you need it.'

Fury drove her to her feet. Like a small dervish, she hurled herself at him, her fingers crooked into claws. *'I do not need help,'* she panted, determined to wipe the indifferent bleakness from his face.

Iron fingers caught her wrists, held her away from him until she whimpered and sagged. He pushed her back on to the seat and said implacably. 'Then don't bother coming back. I don't want to see you again until you can prove that you've freed yourself from the hangover of your marriage.'

Icy tears began to track down her face. Had she been so wilfully stupid as to fall in love with another man who wasn't satisfied with her, who wanted her to prove herself over and over again?

'In the meantime, go back to Auckland,' he told her. 'You've done enough damage here.'

Slowly her hands crept towards him in the classic pleading position. She didn't care; nor did she care that the light of the stars must reveal the anguish in her expression. She only knew that she had to explain what had gone wrong in her marriage before it was impossible

for her to do so. 'You've got it all wrong,' she cried.
'Alick, please——'

But he wasn't listening. 'You used me as a substitute.
I suppose it has to be the greatest insult one human being
can offer another,' he said bitingly.

'No!' If it hadn't been so horrifying, that would be
funny!

'Yes, and because I wanted you more than I've ever
wanted anyone else, I thought I could endure it.' He
watched as her pleading hands drooped, came back to
cover her face from his merciless gaze. 'But I'm not a
masochist, Laurel. Come back when you can convince
me that you want *me*, not a replacement for the man
who walked out on you and left you aching for more.'

She got up and walked across the terrace, through the
house and across the silver and ebony expanse of the
orchard, ignoring the eager snuffling of a hedgehog and
the flutter of wings as she disturbed a bird by stumbling
sightlessly into an orange tree.

Not in her worst nightmares had she experienced such
pain. From some ancient source of wisdom deep inside
she knew that she would not be able to survive if she
gave in to it; to get through the next few days she was
going to have to cut herself in two, and ignore the
bleeding creature crouched in the ruins of her dreams.

She managed. She even managed to say goodbye to
Alick the next morning. Her sleepless night showed in
her drawn pallor, but he didn't look any different; the
inflexible angles and planes of his face were as disciplined as ever, his smile as dazzling. Perhaps it was only
she who noticed that his eyes were cold and empty,
opaque as a sterile sea on some dead planet.

The rest of the summer was beastly, sticky and hot, the
air pressing down on to the city with leaden weight,
mingling in a diabolical cocktail with car fumes and
brazen sunlight, creating days when the only relief was

to drive to one of Auckland's magnificent beaches for a long, crowded soak in the water.

Laurel was working hard; she had contracted to produce four book reviews each week for one of the newspapers, and was still chasing articles. Her supervisor had put several other bits of work her way and she had found more opportunities through the grapevine that university graduates could tap into. She had what she considered a modest success; her mother referred to her as a journalist, and she was beginning to think of herself as one. She had even sent off a manuscript for one of the new primary school primers and had heard back informally that chances were it would be accepted.

Her thesis, checked one last time, was handed to the binder then delivered, in the glory of a dark blue cover and gold lettering, to her supervisor. Laurel thought wearily that if anyone had told her six months ago that she could hand it in with no more than a mild interest in its final evaluation she would have found it difficult to conceive of such a situation. Nevertheless, it was true.

Sometimes she thought that it was just as well that her career path was so promising, because her personal life was a desert.

Oh, she managed to exist. She didn't smile much unless her mother was around, and she found some solace in her work; at least it stopped her mind from repeating in slow, loving replay every second of every time she had seen Alick, heard him, felt him ...

And the bitter, deadly aftermath.

How could he believe that her sighs, her kisses, her surrender to that overwhelming ecstasy, were all for a dead man? How could he believe that she was locked into some obscene sort of dependency on Martin? It seemed so unlike her arrogant, confident Alick, so at variance with what she knew of him.

But then, how good was she at reading men's characters? She had certainly misread Martin's; why shouldn't she be as wrong about Alick, too?

And her mind would return to its treadmill, endlessly wondering what was wrong with her that she couldn't form a satisfying relationship with a man.

But only for a short time. She knew now that it was impossible for her to keep grieving and stay sane, so she told herself sternly that she would have to drag herself out of this swampy morass of self-pity and keep going. Strength lay in a kind of stern endurance. Alick had shown her that although he could take her to heaven in his arms he had no place for her in his heart, so she had a living to earn and a life to lead without him.

But oh, it still stung with an excruciating, never-ending pain, the fact that he had only made love to her because of pique at her insult. She should have known that telling him she wanted him only because he looked like Martin would wound his touchy male pride. She knew, none better, the sort of cruelty a man could indulge in to appease his ego. But it was agony to realise that Alick had chosen to salvage his pride in a way that had shattered hers forever.

And she wept because, although she loved him, she despised him.

Letters from Sophie arrived for her mother; Mrs Webster read small parts of them out to Laurel, carefully, Laurel guessed, avoiding any reference to Alick. She did, however, say with highly suspect off-handedness, 'Sophie thinks that Jenna and Alick are seeing each other again. She says Jenna is looking radiant, but no one can read Alick's thoughts.'

It was like a clean death-blow, rather than the slow bleeding to death Laurel had been enduring. So Jenna, pretty, innocent, loving, dependent Jenna, had won. She had better, Laurel thought grimly, make him happy. And Alick had better make her happy, too.

In a way that letter marked a turning-point. The weather was still as hard to bear, the pain in her heart as great, but the definite termination to her dreams meant that she could stop hoping and turn her mind to living without Alick, without love. Laurel accepted an invitation to a concert and discovered that she enjoyed the evening, the music, and the company of the man she went with.

He took her for coffee and a drink afterwards, and when he had delivered her to the door suggested another evening out, this time to see an avant-garde film at the university. Without hesitation she accepted. His mouth, when he kissed her, was warm and gentle, and she accepted that, too.

The next morning she went into Queen Street to interview a woman who had sold raffle tickets in the same small booth for over fifty years, but who was being forced to give up by the advent of Lotto and other more efficient methods of parting gamblers from their money.

It turned out to be a highly entertaining exercise, one in which both participants enjoyed themselves very much, and when at last Laurel set off up the sticky street to her bus-stop she felt that subtle but overpowering tingle that told her she was going to sell the article. Smiling, she had almost reached the stop when she thought she saw Alick's wide shoulders and proudly poised head.

Heat suffused her body, followed swiftly by a convulsive shudder. She knew that it wouldn't be him. This happened occasionally: a glimpse of someone who bore a faint superficial resemblance, followed by a suffocating leap of her heart, an acute physical response.

But this man did more than just look like Alick, he moved like him too, walking up the street with that smooth predator's stride, the sun gleaming amber-gold in his hair.

When he got to the bus-stop he stopped and stood back, turning a little. At the sight of that arrogant slash of profile her heart stopped beating in her breast.

Why now? she thought despairingly, as the crowd eddied past her. New Zealand's population was so small that coincidences like this were inevitable, but why now?

Pride wouldn't let her slink away like a criminal. Setting her mouth she walked on, neither hurrying nor slowing down, her eyes shadowed by her lashes. Several women assessed him openly as they came near, not put off by the barely hidden impatience marking his autocratic features. Jealousy rose acrid in Laurel's throat as she marked the subtle signs of their appreciation.

Although she kept her eyes on the footpath she knew the instant he caught sight of her. The hair on the back of her neck lifted in a primitive warning.

He looked taut and dangerous, the lean lines of his face expressing a savage restlessness, heavy lids narrowing his eyes. Lithely he moved through the crowd to take her elbow in a grip that made her wince and pull away.

Instantly it eased, but there was no evading him. 'Your mother told me you might be here,' he said brusquely. 'I have to speak to you.'

Laurel frowned. 'I don't know what about,' she said in a stifled voice, keeping her face averted. She read envy in another woman's eyes and thought tiredly, If only you knew the sort of man he is!

'You didn't think we'd said all we had to say to each other, now, did you?' His voice was coldly mocking.

Instinctively she pulled away again but his fingers held her imprisoned. Laurel stiffened, aware of people staring, of smiles and smirks and several concerned looks.

'Let me go,' she spat, tugging fruitlessly.

'No.' With implacable ease he set off up a side-street, dragging her with him, his features carved in lines of complete determination. Her heart twisted; painfully, she noted the signs of strain in his face, the deepening of lines in the striking, unhandsome face, the sharper etching of jaw and mouth.

'Alick,' she protested, trying to dig her heels in. Then, as he ignored her completely, 'How's Jenna?'

'Unhappy, but that is not your concern.'

'It's yours, though.'

He stopped and looked down at her, searching her face. 'In the sense that I made her unhappy, yes. In the sense that I'm responsible for her happiness, no. It's over. She understands that now.'

'But Aunt Sophie told Mum...' She stopped, for triumph gleamed with a cold light in the steel-blue depths of his eyes.

'She was wrong,' he said curtly. 'Jenna has a new job in Tauranga; she's already left Kerikeri. Laurel, I've got the car parked in a friend's basement. Come with me and we'll go to the Domain and talk. If you want to go home after that, I'll take you.'

She hesitated, weighing the cost. Trust came hard to her, but after a moment she nodded. His grip tightened; he bent and kissed her hot brow, and without saying anything more turned to urge her up the street.

The 'friend's basement' turned out to be a car park beneath one of the tall buildings that formed the financial quarter, and Alick's big Jaguar was parked next door to a Rolls-Royce in the directors' area.

Laurel sat down in the smooth leather seat and waited while he set the car in motion; she looked sightlessly out at the crowded streets for the five minutes it took to get them to the Domain, a lovely grassy spot that had once been a volcanic crater, the seaward wall of which was now crowned by the magnificent Greek Revival Museum, a memorial from a grateful people to the dead of two World Wars.

People debouched shrilly from tour buses and more dotted the limp green grass, but there were few about where Alick switched off the engine in the shade of the huge buttresses of a Moreton Bay figtree.

Laurel stared straight ahead. Across the wide expanse of mown grass a little boy ran away from his mother, his teasing laughter like small chimes in the warm air as his chubby legs pumped furiously.

'Sophie was wrong,' Alick said at last, his voice level and without emotion. 'I've seen Jenna once since you left, and then only because she came to the house. Unfortunately Sophie called in while she was there. She misunderstood the reason for her visit.'

She had no right to ask but she had to know. 'What did Jenna want?'

'She'd heard that I wasn't seeing you and she wanted to know whether there was any future for us. I said no, and she wept a little, called me a few names I richly deserve, and left.'

Silence. She asked quietly, 'Would you have married her if I hadn't come along?'

He shrugged. 'Possibly.'

Pain etched a white line around her mouth. 'Why, Alick?'

Heavily, he said, 'About three years ago a couple settled in Kerikeri. They had been married when they were both very young, and—well, to cut a long story short, she developed an infatuation for me. Unfortunately, although she did her best to hide it he sensed what was happening, but instead of fighting for her he got out, acting like a noble idiot.'

Michelle. It had to be her. Swallowing the bitter jealousy that clogged her throat, Laurel asked huskily, 'Did you have an affair with her?'

'No.' The word cracked through the stridulations of the cicadas in the tree above them. 'When she came to her senses she realised that she truly loved her husband and very wisely went after him. They're back together again, although they're no longer living in Kerikeri. But I felt responsible.'

'Why?' she asked quietly.

'I was physically attracted to her. She was very beautiful, and if she'd been single, and willing, I'd have enjoyed making love to her. But I was not in love with her. The whole thing left me with a distinctly unpleasant taste in my mouth, and a grave suspicion of physical attraction and the intense but fleeting emotions it gives rise to.'

She understood now. 'So that's why you chose Jenna.'

'Yes. She was so open, so much in love with me, sweet and safe. And in a way I loved her. I told myself that that would be enough, that if I'd been going to fall in love I'd have done it by then, so I was quite ready to marry her, take what she had to offer and give her what I could. I was bloody arrogant.'

His mouth twisted. 'I thought she'd be happy enough with the affection and the lukewarm passion I felt for her. But it didn't take me long to realise that even if Jenna was happy with what we had, I wasn't. However, it was too late. We were engaged and I owed her my loyalty. Then you came, and after one look I knew that nothing was ever going to be the same again. But there was your marriage. Apparently,' with a barely hidden sneer, 'it had been made in heaven, yet within a year he had left you——'

She said unsteadily, '*I* left *Martin* because I could see that we weren't ever going to be happy.'

'But——'

'He couldn't bear rejection,' she interrupted, the words dragging. 'He had to save his face, so he told everyone that he had been the one to go. I'm surprised Mum didn't tell you that.'

His mouth tightened forbiddingly, a tiny pulse flicking in his jaw. 'She told me very little, and that only reluctantly. Why did you leave Du Fresne?'

She lowered her lashes, staring unseeingly at the sunlit grass and the huge white bulk of the museum up on the hill. It was very hot; tiny beads of moisture popped out across her top lip and at her temples. In a swift sideways glance her eyes travelled down the unforgiving strength of his profile, marking the stark framework of bones that gave him his aura of implacable power.

She said on a defeated sigh, 'I left him because I was useless in bed.' Her mouth twisted in painful irony. 'He was very sensual, and I wasn't. As you can imagine, it was not a good situation. So I left him.'

Fascinated, she watched as his head swivelled sharply. His eyes blazed like blue-black sapphires. 'What the hell do you mean? You went up in flames in my arms, you gave yourself to me with such sweet passion that it still aches in me now. Useless in bed! God, if you were any more *sensual* we'd have set the bloody waterfall on fire.'

Her mouth trembled, for however good she had been he had still sent her away. 'It was you,' she whispered. 'I wasn't—like that—with him.'

'Then he was a poor lover.'

She bit her lip. 'No. He had had quite a few relationships—he s-said that he had never not satisfied a woman before me.'

The tell-tale stutter horrified her, but he said blankly, 'And you believed him?'

'I—yes.'

Irony pulled the thin mouth a little lop-sided. 'Had you ever slept with anyone else?'

'No,' she blurted, then could have sunk into the ground.

'So you were a pushover, a chaste, inexperienced twenty-year-old, in love with love, in the throes of your first physical infatuation, only too easy to convince that you were to blame for not being aroused by a selfish lover.' He spoke judicially, in a calm measured voice that bewildered her.

'You don't know that he was selfish.'

'I do know it. You were too startled when we kissed—it was obvious that you weren't accustomed to being approached with any finesse. I noticed, but when I should have found the reason for your reaction I let my conviction that you were still in love with him throw me off the track.'

His voice was filled with derision directed at himself. He held her wide gaze with an intent, unsmiling look.

'And you have such experience, I suppose,' she said, striving for a healthy sarcasm, 'that every woman swoons in ecstasy in your arms.'

He lifted a devastating brow and drawled, 'I don't know about that—I haven't made love with every woman, but those I have had seemed satisfied by the experience. Tell me, Laurel, have you ever made love with anybody other than your husband? After you left him?'

'No. No, I haven't.' Colour rushed through the pale heart of her face.

'In that case, you really had no idea whether or not you could respond normally to the promptings of your own body.'

She said quietly, 'I was too frightened to experiment or—Martin used to call me frigid and I—and I—I thought there was something wrong with me.'

He didn't touch her but his hand clenched on the wheel as he swore, fluently and without repeating himself, for several minutes, calling a man who was dead names she had never heard in the flat monotone of extreme rage.

At length he reined in his anger and said savagely, 'God, no wonder you didn't want anything to do with me. No wonder you tried everything you could to keep me at arm's length! I wish to hell I'd taken more notice of what was staring me in the eye, instead of letting my bloody arrogant pride get in the way. When you said that the only reason you wanted me was because I looked like him, I could have killed you.'

'So you decided to salvage your pride and punish me,' she said without expression.

He said between his teeth, 'Is that what you think? That I punished you for saying that by making love to you?'

'It seemed logical,' she said cautiously, afraid as she had never been before. 'You—made it fairly obvious— afterwards—that you didn't want me again.'

His anger was a palpable thing, a force out of control. But even as she shrank back he mastered it again, turning away to look out through the windscreen at the little boy, who was now playing 'Ring O' Roses' with his mother.

After a moment he said in the soft level voice that so intimidated her, 'I can see why you came to that conclusion, but it's wrong. I made love to you because I wasn't able to stop myself. I knew that you weren't ready for it, that it was the wrong time, but you smiled at me and I would have died to have you.'

Tears blurred her eyes. She had to believe him.

He waited a moment, but when she said nothing he continued, 'At first, like you, I thought that it was physical. I was certain it was the same kind of madness that had ruined Michelle's marriage, only for me it was much more intense. But I expected it to be just as evanescent. And I was sure that it was just sexual attraction for you, too. That was reinforced when you flung the fact that I looked like Martin in my teeth. You did it to hurt, didn't you?'

Ashamed, she nodded. 'But mainly as a defence. I was too conscious of you. I wanted to protect myself; I suppose I knew that you'd take it as an insult.'

His smile was narrow and hard. 'How well you read me! When I realised at your friend Sarah's party that this bloody need that was eating through my heart and mind and body wasn't going to go away, that I didn't just want you, I was in love with you, I knew I had to make you realise that it was me you wanted now, not a pale replica of your husband. So I put the idea of inviting you up for Christmas into Sophie's mind, and called off the engagement to Jenna.'

Laurel made a soft little sound and he said harshly, 'Yes, it wasn't easy. I let her down as gently as I could, but I behaved like a swine to her. Then you and your mother came, and although you looked at me with suspicion I knew that I'd done the right thing. I also knew that I was going to have to proceed cautiously. I couldn't just sweep you off your feet and into my heart, which was what I wanted to do. So I wooed you, let you see what sort of person I am, shoved this damned ache on the back-burner as far as I could, all so that you wouldn't be so hung-up on my physical attributes. And then we made love. It was the most magnificent thing that had ever happened to me, even though I cursed myself for letting it happen when I knew you weren't ready for it.'

'Then why...?' she cried, mouth quivering as her eyes filled. 'Why did you send me away so brutally?'

'Hush, my dearest heart, don't cry, please don't cry.' He took her hands, holding them to his mouth, and when she had gulped back some of her self-control he went on unsteadily, 'You made it obvious that you resented this wildfire passion as much as I did, but I thought it was because Martin had left you, that you still loved him. I knew that if I couldn't get you to see me, rather than a dead man, then we had no future together.'

His eyes burned, devouring her. 'Because I couldn't be satisfied with second best. I wanted you to discover that it was *me* you wanted, *me* you ached for, *me* you surrendered to when we made love, not some ghost in your mind. I couldn't think of any other way of doing it except by staying away from you until you realised just how much you needed me. If only I'd known that he had brutalised you to that degree, I'd have gone about things in an entirely different way.'

'You said—I was sick,' she said thickly.

His hands tightened on hers. 'I wanted to make you think, to recognise what you were doing to yourself. I hoped—oh, God, I suppose it was partly black jealousy, too. The thought of you giving him what you had just given me made me furious and bitter, like a cuckolded husband. It's irrational, but that was how I felt. I wanted everything, and he had stolen some of your life.'

'I thought you'd—had what you wanted,' she said, aware that she should be happy, yet unable to relax enough to achieve happiness. 'I felt——'

'Betrayed,' he supplied starkly. 'I had everything so wrong. It must have seemed like the most arrant betrayal. I'm sorry, my love, my little heart, my sweetest soul.'

'You weren't to know,' she said quietly. She leaned forwards and touched his cheek, holding her breath at her daring, her finger shaking with pleasure that was close to a pain as it traced the dark curve of rough silk. Tears ached at the back of her throat. 'I missed you.'

He held her hand there, his eyes heated and deep and mysterious as they pinned hers. 'I'm sorry,' he said.

'It's all right. I can see why you sent me away, even though I thought I was going to die with the pain and the wanting. And I think perhaps you were right, even if you did it for the wrong reasons. I was so confused, I needed these last weeks to banish Martin to where he belongs, safely in the past where he can never hurt me again. And to realise that you and he are not in the least alike.' Sensation, as inevitable and beautiful as the spring thaw, began to run through the hidden subliminal pathways of her being. She said quietly, 'What do we do now?'

'We go home and tell your anxious mother that everything is all right. Then I ring home and tell them.' He smiled with glittering anticipation. 'They'll be mightily relieved; I've been in a cold rage since you left. Not that it will be any great surprise to any of them. They all know how I feel about you. That first night you spent at the homestead, Gran warned me about my attitude. She was worried because she'd sensed how I felt about Jenna and she saw the impact you made on me. She didn't think I should accept second best when the real thing was so shining bright.'

'So that's what . . .' She stopped, then at his enquiring glance told him what she had overheard from the stairs, ending, 'I thought she was warning you that I was—available.'

'I see. He watched the little boy, now rolling joyously across the grass, his laughter ringing in the air. 'What a very poor self-image you have, my darling. In a way

I'm sorry that that damned puppy killed himself. I'd like to have told him a few home truths.' His voice was soft but lethal. 'No, Gran was trying to convince me that instant attraction was not necessarily a bad thing. She knew, you see. She was going to marry a nice safe man, a man she loved in a calm peaceful way, but fortunately your grandmother ran away with him. Then Gran met Grandy, and she realised how close she had come to disaster. She thought I might end up the same way.'

'She's very wise.' She had to ask it. 'How—how is Jenna?'

His expression was set in lines of pain and self-contempt. 'She's hurt, but—she's going out with a young man who will, I think, eventually take her mind off the fact that she's been jilted.'

She bit her lip. 'I'm sorry. I never wanted to hurt her.'

'Neither did I. The fault was all mine, however, none of yours. I chose her. At least I never slept with her.'

'But she said...'

He waited a second then asked, 'What did she say? And when?'

So she told him of Jenna's visit to Auckland and that painful, awkward interview. She didn't need to tell him how much the incident had strengthened her decision to have nothing to do with him, because she read his comprehension in his face.

The hard mouth tightened. 'I see. I can't blame her for using all the weapons she had at her disposal. When she grows up a little she's going to be quite a woman.'

It was ignoble to feel a pang of jealousy, but Laurel did. Staring down at the hands tightly linked together in her lap, she wondered why they were still sitting here in the car, talking.

'So, what happens now?' she asked at last, when it seemed he was in no hurry to break the tense silence.

'That's entirely up to you,' he said, his voice incredibly remote. 'If you still feel that this is a purely physical thing for you, I'll accept that. For the time being, anyway.'

She must have made a muffled sound of surprise because he turned on her, the steel-sheen of his eyes cold enough to burn through to her soul, his features drawn and hostile.

'Yes, I know that I said I couldn't be satisfied with second best, but this last month has proved to me that I'll take whatever I can get from you,' he said harshly. 'If it's just sex, well, I can live with that for a time. But I warn you, I'm going to do my damnedest to change your mind. I love you. I want to marry you. And if I ever catch you looking sideways at any other man of my build and colouring, I'll make sure you never do it again.'

As proposals went it was a far cry from Martin's, which had been conducted to the accompaniments of roses and wine and sweet music, all the clichéd romantic accoutrements. Laurel knew which she preferred. Her heart began to sing, the sizzling incandescence overlaid by a warm tenderness that was new to her, and oddly stimulating.

'Of course I'll marry you,' she said softly. 'I've been *in* love with you since I first set eyes on you, and I've *loved* you since about three days later. As for all the stupid guff I spouted about physical types—I think that was a valiant rearguard action. I've finally woken up to the fact that there are actually quite a few men of your height and colouring in this world, and the only one I've fallen in love with was you. I was carried away by romantic dreams when I married Martin; I think I fell for him because he looked like you.'

He showed his teeth. 'Bloody fool. He caused you so much pain.'

'He was just as much deceived as I was,' she said, able to be generous now. 'He thought I'd be the sort of wife his mother was, always putting him first, making sure that he was definitely the head of the family; and when he discovered that I wasn't prepared to give up my interests and my work for him he just tried to turn me into the sort of wife he needed.'

'He hurt you, used you as a whipping-boy for his own failure,' he said tightly.

'He's dead now, Alick, and we are very much alive.'

He had listened with a set face and narrowed eyes, but at this last observation the muscles relaxed, and he smiled, the tenderness she had glimpsed only rarely very much to the fore. 'So you are over it?'

'Yes.' She smiled back, but said evenly, 'I'll always be sorry I married him. He didn't get much joy out of me, poor Martin, and I suppose I'll always feel that in some way I betrayed you by marrying him; but it's over, it's in the past. I love you.'

He moved her hand to his mouth, strong fingers holding it there while he kissed the palm, the swift touch of his tongue setting pulses throbbing through her. 'If he didn't get any joy from you it was because he was bloody clumsy,' he said, his hard voice at variance with the sensual little caress.

'Oh, no, he was experienced...' She stopped, colouring slightly.

Alick's eyes were steady, burning with a clear angry flame that wasn't directed at her. 'Laurel, he might have slept with a hundred women, but did you ever ask *them* how he made love? He sounds like the sort of selfish, clumsy idiot who takes what he wants and has no interest in pleasuring his partner. You and I have made love together, remember? And you are not frigid. You responded with a blazing heat that set me alight as no other woman has been able to do, and you gave so generously, so ardently, that it burned me up completely. And you enjoyed it, didn't you?'

'I don't think enjoy is quite the word.' Her voice wobbled and she looked down at their hands, linked together. 'I went right out of my mind, as you must know.'

His teeth showed in a purely masculine grin. 'Yes, I did notice.' Suddenly sobering, he looked intently at her and said with crisp authority, 'So no more about being frigid. You were abused by a brutally clumsy lover but that's all in the past. He had his chance and he lost it.'

Chilled by the ruthless note in the words, she looked at him. He made no attempt to soften his expression, contempt for Martin very clear on the striking, angular face. Her eyes were troubled but she accepted that he was a hard man, and that he was not going to change. If she loved him, if she married him, she would have to accept him as he was, not some sort of romanticised fantasy she had made of him. She had done that once, transforming a selfish immature man into the lover she had longed for. If she took Alick, it must be with her eyes open.

Her gaze cleared, became warm and melting. 'All right,' she said.

He touched her trembling mouth with a lean finger. 'I'll take you home now,' he said softly. 'Your mother is waiting for us.'

Disappointment must have showed fleetingly in her face, for he laughed and put her hand back in her lap. 'Of course, we could ring her from my flat,' he said, smiling, allowing the passion to show in his eyes as they lingered on the soft contours of her mouth. 'It's not too far away from here, and it's very private. When can we get married?'

She looked a little startled, then suggested, tongue in cheek, 'In a week's time?'

Dark glints of amusement and passion showed beneath his lashes. 'I might just last out,' he said. 'In the meantime, why don't we go back to my flat and I can show you in one of the many delicious ways there are just how much I love you?'

Radiance broke through her expression. She slanted a wicked glance at him, amusement tucking in the corners of her mouth. 'All right,' she said demurely. She leaned over and pressed a kiss to his lean hand. 'I love you,' she said softly, the words a vow. 'For the rest of my life.'

His hands were trembling as they framed her face. 'Dear heart,' he said reverently. 'For the rest of our lives together.'

HARLEQUIN
Romance®

HARLEQUIN ROMANCE
LOVES BABIES!

And next month's title in

THE BRIDAL COLLECTION

brings you *two* babies—and, of course, a wedding.

BOTH OF THEM
by Rebecca Winters

THE BRIDE objected.
THE GROOM insisted.
THE WEDDING was for the children's sake!

Available this month in
THE BRIDAL COLLECTION

LOVE YOUR ENEMY
by Ellen James

Harlequin Romance #3202
Available wherever
Harlequin Books are sold.

OVER THE YEARS, TELEVISION HAS BROUGHT
THE LIVES AND LOVES OF MANY CHARACTERS INTO
YOUR HOMES. NOW HARLEQUIN INTRODUCES YOU
TO THE TOWN AND PEOPLE OF

One small town—twelve terrific love stories.

GREAT READING…GREAT SAVINGS…
AND A FABULOUS FREE GIFT!

Each book set in Tyler is a self-contained love story; together, the
twelve novels stitch the fabric of the community.

By collecting proofs-of-purchase found in each Tyler book, you can
receive a fabulous gift, ABSOLUTELY FREE! And use our special
Tyler coupons to save on your next TYLER book purchase.

Join us for the fifth TYLER book,
BLAZING STAR by Suzanne Ellison, available in July.

Is there really a murder cover-up?
Will Brick and Karen overcome differences and find true love?

Coming Next Month

#1471 WHEN THE DEVIL DRIVES Sara Craven
Joanna knows there'll be a day of reckoning between herself and Cal Blackstone.
And it means she'll have to make a tough decision because Cal holds all the
best cards. If she refuses his demands, her family will suffer—but the price he
wants her to pay is far too high.

#1472 THE SEDUCTION OF KEIRA Emma Darcy
When Keira returns to Australia, her cousin welcomes her with open arms. It
seems he needs her to seduce a rival. Keira agrees to do her best, but before
she has the chance, she meets Nick Sarazan, the man of her dreams. And he
loses no time in seducing Keira.

#1473 NIGHTS OF DESIRE Natalie Fox
Carrie comes to Spain to look for a missing boyfriend and finds Alex Drayton
instead. Soon she's working for him, then she's dreaming about him. Carrie
knows it's only a matter of time before he becomes her entire world....

#1474 AN UNEQUAL PARTNERSHIP Rosemary Gibson
Mike refuses to abandon the airline business her grandfather built—especially
to a cold, calculating businessman like Luke Duncan. Luke is not a man who's
easily thwarted, but perhaps it's time he's taught a few of life's lessons.

#1475 RISK OF THE HEART Grace Green
Capri is determined to avoid her father's heavy-handed matchmaking
attempts and have a real holiday this year. For a short while, maybe she can
have some fun, instead of spending all her time fighting off rich admirers.
Then she meets Taggart Smith—a man who changes everything!

#1476 SECOND TIME LOVING Penny Jordan
Daniel Forbes is attractive and charming, and he's made it clear he's attracted
to Angelica. But after a bad experience with gold digger Giles, Angelica has
vowed not to let another man make a fool of her. But, try as she might, she
finds Daniel impossible to resist.

#1477 DARK GUARDIAN Rebecca King
Stranded on a desert island with the mysterious Brand Carradine is not as
romantic as it sounds. At least that's Fliss's first reaction to her predicament.
After all, Brand is her legal guardian!

#1478 NO WAY TO BEGIN Michelle Reid
Nina despises Anton Lakitos. She's convinced that the arrogant Greek property
developer's interest in the family business has ruined her father's health.
That's not her only problem. Anton is hell-bent on acquiring Nina, too—even if
he has to use blackmail to do so.

Available in July wherever paperback books are sold, or through
Harlequin Reader Service:

In the U.S.
P.O. Box 1397
Buffalo, NY
14240-1397

In Canada
P.O. Box 603
Fort Erie, Ontario
L2A 5X3

BIG SUMMER READ

Summer Reading
At Its Best

In July, Harlequin and Silhouette bring readers the Big Summer Read Program. Heat up your summer with these four exciting new novels by top Harlequin and Silhouette authors.

SOMEWHERE IN TIME by Barbara Bretton
YESTERDAY COMES TOMORROW by Rebecca Flanders
A DAY IN APRIL by Mary Lynn Baxter
LOVE CHILD by Patricia Coughlin

From time travel to fame and fortune, this program offers something for everyone.

Available at your favorite retail outlet.

BSR

H A R L E Q U I N
American Romance®

American Romance's yearlong celebration continues. Join your favorite authors as they celebrate love set against the special times each month throughout 1992.

Next month, fireworks light up the sky when Anne Haynes and John Westfield meet in a special Fourth of July romance:

#445
HOME FREE
by Cathy Gillen Thacker

Read all the books in *A Calendar of Romance*, coming to you one per month all year, only in American Romance.

"GET AWAY FROM IT ALL" SWEEPSTAKES

HERE'S HOW THE SWEEPSTAKES WORKS

NO PURCHASE NECESSARY

To enter each drawing, complete the appropriate Official Entry Form or a 3" by 5" index card by hand-printing your name, address and phone number and the trip destination that the entry is being submitted for (i.e., Caneel Bay, Canyon Ranch or London and the English Countryside) and mailing it to: Get Away From It All Sweepstakes, P.O. Box 1397, Buffalo, New York 14269-1397.

No responsibility is assumed for lost, late or misdirected mail. Entries must be sent separately with first class postage affixed, and be received by: 4/15/92 for the Caneel Bay Vacation Drawing, 5/15/92 for the Canyon Ranch Vacation Drawing and 6/15/92 for the London and the English Countryside Vacation Drawing. Sweepstakes is open to residents of the U.S. (except Puerto Rico) and Canada, 21 years of age or older as of 5/31/92.

For complete rules send a self-addressed, stamped (WA residents need not affix return postage) envelope to: Get Away From It All Sweepstakes, P.O. Box 4892, Blair, NE 68009.

© 1992 HARLEQUIN ENTERPRISES LTD.   SWP-RLS

"GET AWAY FROM IT ALL" SWEEPSTAKES

HERE'S HOW THE SWEEPSTAKES WORKS

NO PURCHASE NECESSARY

To enter each drawing, complete the appropriate Official Entry Form or a 3" by 5" index card by hand-printing your name, address and phone number and the trip destination that the entry is being submitted for (i.e., Caneel Bay, Canyon Ranch or London and the English Countryside) and mailing it to: Get Away From It All Sweepstakes, P.O. Box 1397, Buffalo, New York 14269-1397.

No responsibility is assumed for lost, late or misdirected mail. Entries must be sent separately with first class postage affixed, and be received by: 4/15/92 for the Caneel Bay Vacation Drawing, 5/15/92 for the Canyon Ranch Vacation Drawing and 6/15/92 for the London and the English Countryside Vacation Drawing. Sweepstakes is open to residents of the U.S. (except Puerto Rico) and Canada, 21 years of age or older as of 5/31/92.

For complete rules send a self-addressed, stamped (WA residents need not affix return postage) envelope to: Get Away From It All Sweepstakes, P.O. Box 4892, Blair, NE 68009.

© 1992 HARLEQUIN ENTERPRISES LTD.   SWP-RLS

"GET AWAY FROM IT ALL"

Brand-new Subscribers-Only Sweepstakes

OFFICIAL ENTRY FORM

This entry must be received by: May 15, 1992
This month's winner will be notified by: May 31, 1992
Trip must be taken between: June 30, 1992—June 30, 1993

YES, I want to win the Canyon Ranch vacation for two. I understand the prize includes round-trip airfare and the two additional prizes revealed in the BONUS PRIZES insert.

Name _____

Address _____

City _____

State/Prov._____ Zip/Postal Code_____

Daytime phone number _____
(Area Code)

Return entries with invoice in envelope provided. Each book in this shipment has two entry coupons — and the more coupons you enter, the better your chances of winning!
© 1992 HARLEQUIN ENTERPRISES LTD.   2M-CPN

"GET AWAY FROM IT ALL"

Brand-new Subscribers-Only Sweepstakes

OFFICIAL ENTRY FORM

This entry must be received by: May 15, 1992
This month's winner will be notified by: May 31, 1992
Trip must be taken between: June 30, 1992—June 30, 1993

YES, I want to win the Canyon Ranch vacation for two. I understand the prize includes round-trip airfare and the two additional prizes revealed in the BONUS PRIZES insert.

Name _____

Address _____

City _____

State/Prov._____ Zip/Postal Code_____

Daytime phone number _____
(Area Code)

Return entries with invoice in envelope provided. Each book in this shipment has two entry coupons — and the more coupons you enter, the better your chances of winning!
© 1992 HARLEQUIN ENTERPRISES LTD.   2M-CPN